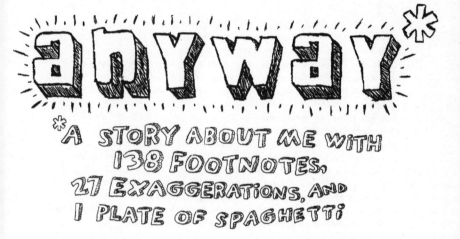

anyway*

*A STORY ABOUT ME WITH 138 FOOTNOTES, 27 EXAGGERATIONS, AND 1 PLATE OF SPAGHETTI

ARTHUR SALM

Simon & Schuster Books for Young Readers
New York   London   Toronto   Sydney   New Delhi

SIMON & SCHUSTER BOOKS FOR YOUNG READERS
An imprint of Simon & Schuster Children's Publishing Division
1230 Avenue of the Americas, New York, New York 10020

SIMON & SCHUSTER BOOKS FOR YOUNG READERS is a trademark of Simon & Schuster, Inc.
For information about special discounts for bulk purchases, please contact
Simon & Schuster Special Sales at 1-866-506-1949 or business@simonandschuster.com.
The Simon & Schuster Speakers Bureau can bring authors to your live event.
For more information or to book an event, contact the Simon & Schuster Speakers Bureau
at 1-866-248-3049 or visit our website at www.simonspeakers.com.
Book design by Dan Potash
The text for this book is set in Goudy Old Style.
Manufactured in the United States of America
0312 FFG
10 9 8 7 6 5 4 3 2 1
Library of Congress Cataloging-in-Publication Data
Salm, Arthur (Arthur Baldauf), 1950–
Anyway* / Arthur Salm. — 1st ed.
p. cm.
"*A story about me with 138 footnotes, 27 exaggerations, and 1 plate of spaghetti."
Summary: At summer camp, twelve-year-old Max reinvents himself
as daring and fearless "Mad Max," and although he regrets some of his behavior among
strangers, he tries to keep some of that fearlessness when he returns home to his friends.
ISBN 978-1-4424-2930-7 (hardcover)
[1. Self-perception—Fiction. 2. Personality—Fiction. 3. Maturation (Psychology)—Fiction.
4. Peer pressure—Fiction. 5. Family life—Fiction. 6. Humorous stories.] I. Title.
PZ7.S15333Any 2012
[Fic]—dc22
2011003491
ISBN 978-1-4424-2932-1 (eBook)

FIRST
EDITION

For three women:
my mother, Henrietta B. Salm,
my wife, Susan Duerksen,
and my daughter, Zoe Duerksen-Salm
. . . who love me anyway

ACKNOWLEDGMENTS

When I was young—I mean, really young—I imagined that someday, when I did the acknowledgments for the book I'd written, I'd thank an editor, maybe, and my wife, if I ever got one. Who else could possibly deserve any credit for a book with my name on it?

Well, kid, I'll tell you.

Anne Marie Welsh was an early reader, when *Anyway** was in a somewhat different form, as were Leigh Fenly, Kelly Mayhew, Clark Brooks, and Daniel Reveles. When at one point I didn't know what to do next, my weekly coffee-and-almond-croissants editor/author pals Zahary Karabashliev and Jennifer de Poyen saved the day, and the manuscript: Zack sent me down the right track and Jennifer kept me from going off the rails. Thanks ten million, guys. Max would say that's an exaggeration, but it's not.

Special thanks to Robin Cruise, who put in a good word—in very good words. Greg Bowerman, a great vet, vetted the dog stuff.

If there are keener, savvier, more understanding . . .

better literary agents than Marietta Zacker and Nancy Gallt, I'd like to hear all about them. Not that I'd believe a word of it.

David Gale, Navah Wolfe, and Dan Potash at Simon & Schuster *got* Max, *got* me . . . *got* the book.

There'd be no *Anyway** if it weren't for my daughter, Zoe Duerksen-Salm, because it began as a short story just for her. She also let me know when I'd written something dumb.

When I left my job at the newspaper, my wife, Susan Duerksen, told me to go ahead and write a book, and not worry about anything. I worried anyway, of course, but what more welcome, more loving words could I hope to hear from my best editor and best friend?

Part One
Tripping[1]

---

1 This is a footnote. <u>Anyway</u>* has 138 of them.
In most books, footnotes are incredibly boring—they
usually just tell you where you can find more boring
stuff to read. The footnotes in this book are different.
You **need** to read them.

chapter

HIGH CAMP; SARA SLUGS AN EXTRATERRESTRIAL; TIME TRIALS

All right, I'm going to tell you this story, and you tell me if you think it's funny. I don't, or at least I didn't at first. But then, I'm the one who sat on the plate of spaghetti.[2]

Anyway, I'm Max. A good kid. Except for the time I decided I didn't want to be a good kid anymore. That's still going on, kind of.

---

2   I just have bad luck with spaghetti. One time I made some to surprise my parents, and it was the most horrible stuff I've ever tasted in my life. They tried to be polite and eat a little of it, but as they chewed they got these really weird looks on their faces and finally they just spit it into their napkins. My mother said, "Max, what did you do to it? All you have to do is put it in boiling water." I said, "You mean the water has to boil first?" My father took out his phone and said, "Pizza or Vietnamese?" I said, "Pizza." They both said, "Vietnamese." I said, "Okay, but with egg noodles," and they got those same weird looks on their faces and said together, "No noodles!" So it was a Vietnamese with brown rice night. Not all my stories have happy endings.

Here's how it started. A few months ago, just before I finished seventh grade, my parents got it into their heads that after school was out for the summer, we had to go to this weeklong family camp in the mountains, just the three of us.[3] They showed me a booklet with pictures of a swimming pool, a gigantic dining hall with a monster fireplace and picnic tables loaded with food, a lake with kayaking and fishing (although my parents made sure not to say the word "fishing"[4]), volleyball courts—about everything you could think of.

"It says there are lots of youth activities," my mom said. The camp really didn't sound too bad, except

---

3 My brother Ben's nineteen and in college now, so he gets out of stuff like that.

4 I've been fishing exactly one time in my life, when this YMCA day camp took us deep-sea fishing. We had to get there so early, the sky was still black. I didn't even know how to bait a hook. A counselor said he'd show me everything, but the boat wasn't even out of the harbor before I started to get seasick, and I basically barfed for the whole four hours. In the middle of it all, I was sitting on a bench with my head between my knees, trying to figure out if moaning helped or made me feel worse. I was also trying to decide whether I was ready to throw up again. A kid sat down next to me and put his head between his knees too, and I thought, At least I'm not the only one. But what he was doing was getting his sack lunch from under the bench. He unwrapped a baloney sandwich and took a big bite. Then he looked over at me. He was chewing with his mouth open. "You look like you're gonna barf again," he said, and he was right.

for the cabin I'd have to share with my parents, and the almost all-day drive to get there.[5] My dad likes to get on the freeway and just *go*, but my mom is always wanting us to go off on little side trips to see stuff. She says it'll only take a few minutes.

"Besides," she says, "we're on vacation. What's the hurry?" They can get pretty mad at each other, especially if we've been in the car for a long time. I'm always on my dad's side, because the stuff my mom wants to see is never interesting,[6] and half the time we can't find it, anyway. And the half the time we do find it, we get lost trying to find our way back to the freeway.

I could tell they'd pretty much made up their minds about the summer camp. And once I found out that we'd be back before Sara Chen's party, I said sure.

I should tell you that even though it's fall now and I've started eighth grade, I'm still only twelve, because my birthday's not till November. That means I'm about the youngest one in my class. As you probably know, that sucks.[7] My parents' friends and my aunts and uncles use the word "tween" a lot. I think they just like saying it, usually right before they tell me how much

5 Car trips are more fun with Alice, but she wouldn't be coming either.

6 I don't mean it's hardly ever interesting. I mean it's *never* interesting.

7 My parents were always telling me not to say "sucks," so I finally stopped saying it around *them*. That's something I learned from Alice: If you're going to break a rule, do it when nobody's around.

I've grown. As if that was news to me. As if I didn't measure myself[8] against the bathroom door every four or five days.

"How do you like being a tween?" they ask, and I tell them I don't know. Then they ask how school is and I say fine, and they ask what grade I'm in and I say eighth, and they say, "Wow! Max is an eighth grader!" And I mean, they all say these same things, word for word.[9]

Anyway, I'd blown it *bad* when Sara, who's been a friend of mine since forever, walked up to me right before history class, just a couple of weeks before school was out for the summer, and asked if I wanted to come to her party at the end of July. I said, "So, you're going to be thirteen, huh?"—even though nobody in the known civilized universe has a girl-boy birthday party after around second grade.

Sara wrinkled her nose and tilted her head and stared at me, like she knew I was an alien but couldn't figure out which planet I was from. Then she laughed and slugged me in the arm. I acted like it didn't hurt, which it did because Sara is a pitcher in a girls' fast-pitch softball league.

"No, *idjit*," she said, still laughing. "It's just a party."

"Oh," I said.

Of course, "Oh" wasn't very cool either, but I was

8 Five feet, ¼ inch, as of thirty seconds ago.

9 There's an official book called 178 Stupid Things to Say to Kids that the government hands out to everyone who manages to live to age twenty-one.

concentrating on getting away from her so that I could rub my arm.[10] So I wasn't being exactly brilliant. But you have to give me a break, because an awful lot of information had been downloaded into my brain in the last few seconds: 1) the party invitation; 2) pain from my left arm; 3) embarrassment at my stupid answer; and 4) noticing Sara's long, very shiny, very black hair, which before I'd always just kind of looked at but now I was liking a lot, and suddenly feeling very uncomfortable about her standing so close.

You've probably picked up on part of my problem already. I start out trying to tell somebody something, like I'm going to tell you about how I sat on the plate of spaghetti,[11] but I get sidetracked because one thought leads me to another and then another. This drives my mom and dad crazy. They'll pester me to tell them something about my day at school, for example. Then, when I do, I end up talking about stuff that, I admit, doesn't have much to do with what I started out talking about. I can see them getting impatient. My mom

---

10 There was definitely going to be a bruise, which would require a better explanation than "A girl hit me." I eventually came up with two: a) "McNaught pushed me into a locker," which would work because Wiley McNaught hates me, and everybody knows it; and b) just shrugging and saying "I don't know" real casually, as if getting bruises was no big deal to a guy like me.

11 It wasn't my fault. You'll see.

gets this really fakey smile.[12] My dad will start glancing down at the newspaper he's holding. Finally one of them will say, "Max, can you just get to the point?"

Anyway,[13] it was going to be a long drive to the camp. As I was helping my dad put our stuff in the car,[14] I started wondering about the kids who'd be there—how I'd get along with them, if any of them would turn out to be good friends, things like that.

Then I got this idea. Nobody at the camp will know me, or know anything about me. Why do I have to act like I always act? Why do I have to be me? *Max, the good boy. Max, the guy nobody pays much attention to.* I mean, why can't I go up there and make myself into a completely different person?

My dad slammed the trunk closed just as my mom walked out the front door and said, "Okay, let's go!" That meant it was time for my dad and me to go back into the house and sit down on the couch. My mom walked back in and said, "What's wrong?" Then she said, "Well, I may as well hit the bathroom before we go." And off she went.

---

12 I just realized that her fakey smile looks exactly like the fakey smile I have in all my school pictures.

13 I end up having to say "Anyway" a lot.

14 He already knew exactly how it would all fit in the trunk. He says he lies in bed the night before a trip and works it out in his head like a giant puzzle. The one time I tried it, I found out that a lot of things aren't the size I thought they were.

"Six minutes," my dad said.

"Eleven," I said.

He looked at his watch and said, "Go!"

We waited. She came out of the bathroom. He looked at his watch again, and said, "We're up to five."

"What?" my mom said. "Oh, sunglasses." Off she went again. Some clattering in the den, then footsteps, then some clattering in the kitchen. "Ready!" she called out. "No, wait—"

"Seven," my dad whispered.

My mom walked to the front door again. "Are we going or not? Come on!"

"Still seven minutes," my dad said. "I'm off by one, you're off by four. I win."

We almost made it to the car, but my mom turned around. "Did you lock the back door?"

"Yup," my dad said.

"Sure?"

"Yeah, yeah. Let's go!" He could see his victory slipping away.

"I'll just check. That way I won't worry about it." And back into the house she went.

I elbowed my father. "Time?"

"I don't know," he said. "I think my watch has stopped."

"I think I won, is what I think," I said.

We stood there leaning against the car.

"I don't think it's my watch," he said. "I think *time* has stopped."

chapter

FOOTNOTES

ave you been reading the footnotes like I asked? Everybody who hasn't been reading the footnotes should go back and read them all right now. The rest of us will wait.

Zzzzzzzzzzzzzzz...

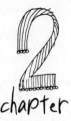
chapter

STRIKEOUT KING; WHY OVERNIGHTS ARE WEIRD; NEW MAX

Is everybody back? Can we go on now? Good. If you pay attention to the first part of a car trip, you think you'll never get anywhere. We were going to drive about 400 miles, and after a mile I said to myself, "We have to do this another 399 times," and it almost made me insane. Then I remembered my idea about becoming a different person, and for the next I-don't-know-how-many miles, I didn't think about how long it was taking. I didn't even notice anything around me. I just stared out the window without seeing anything, and concentrated on who I wanted to be. On *how* I wanted to be.

I'd already been a different person, once, when I was a star pitcher. That's the best accident that ever happened to me.

The thing is, I'm just an okay baseball player. About average, I guess. But last summer—I mean summer of last year, not the summer that just ended—I completely messed up in Little League tryouts,[15] and even though I was eleven, I had to play in the minors again, which is almost all nine- and ten-year-olds. When my friend Evan heard what happened, he said that it sucked.[16]

But I was having the best time of my life.

As I said, I'm an okay player. I know how to catch a ball, I can hit, well, a little, and I've got a pretty good arm. And now I was an eleven-year-old playing against nine- and ten-year-olds. When our coach saw me throw, he said, "Son, how would you like to be a pitcher?"[17]

There was no way those younger kids could hit my fastball. They'd swing and miss, and swing and miss, and swing and miss. Or they'd stand there with the bat on their shoulders, terrified, praying I wouldn't

---

15 What happened was, they had fielding drills first, and a ground ball hit a rock or something and took a really bad hop and glanced off the top of my glove and smashed into my nose. I didn't cry or anything, but it bled like crazy, and by the time it stopped and I got cleaned up, they were through with fielding and I'd missed my turn for the batting part. I had to grab the first bat I saw and run up to the plate without even taking any practice swings. I swung and missed three straight pitches, and tryouts were over. "The exact same thing happened to A-Rod when he was a kid," my dad said when I told him about it.

16 If Evan ever said "sucked" in front of his parents, he'd be grounded till he was forty-six.

17 In the entire history of baseball no one has ever answered "no" to that question.

hit them. Sometimes I'd pretend that some girls from school, maybe Sara and her friend Allie, were watching, but do you know when the last time was that a girl came to a Little League game? Seven hundred years ago. Do you know when the last time was that a girl came to a *minor league* game? Eight hundred years ago.

I'd never been a star before, in anything. Now everybody on the team wanted to hang out with me. Usually before our game there was another game or two, so I'd say, "Let's go to 7-Eleven," and everybody would say, "Yeah! Let's go!" We'd walk over and get Izzes and SoBes,[18] then come back and watch the other games.

---

18 That was just last year, when it was still a big deal for me to go into a store and buy stuff. There's a café a few blocks from our house, where my parents go to drink coffee and read. I like to go with just my dad, because he always ends up letting me have an ice-cream smoothie or a giant chocolate-chip cookie. He'll say, "Now, don't go begging me for something ridiculously sweet, because the answer is going to be no." But when we get there, I know that he can't wait to sit down and start reading, and that he really doesn't want one of our I-Want-This,-Well,-You-Can't-Have-It arguments. So I get the smoothie or the cookie. One Sunday morning I asked if he wanted to walk to the café, and he said, "Not today. But why don't you call a friend to meet you there?" and he handed me a five-dollar bill. Evan got there the same time I did. The woman behind the counter had tattoos all the way up her left arm, but none on her right. She smiled and treated us just like any other customers. We split a hot chocolate and a chocolate-chip muffin, and I gave her the five-dollar bill and then dropped the change into the tip jar. Evan and I sat at an outdoor table. That morning at the café was when I stopped feeling like I was a little kid.

And I was the big guy—I was the one everybody was trying to impress. They all wanted me to like them.

Hey, I knew it wasn't fair. For a while I didn't let myself think about it. I'd be riding home in the car after pitching another great game, and I'd remember that the other kids were all nine and ten, while I was eleven. But I'd just push the thought away.[19]

That kind of worked, but even if I wasn't actually thinking about it, it started bothering me. Like having a guilty conscience, I guess, even though I hadn't done anything wrong. So one day I rode my bike all the way to the Little League field and just sat there, right behind the backstop, balancing myself by holding on to the chain-link fence with my pitching hand. I stared out at the empty field, and here's what I came up with:

It's true that I'm bigger and faster and stronger than just about everybody else in the league, but wait a minute. What about the guys my age who are bigger and faster and stronger than me? That's not fair either. But then, as my dad is always reminding me, Life Isn't Fair. And this time, Life Isn't Being Fair to a whole bunch of nine- and ten-year-olds.

I didn't *mean* to screw up in the tryouts so that I could be a star. It just happened. So I decided I could deal with the unfairness. Go ahead—ask me if I feel bad about it.[20]

---

19 Sometimes I do the same thing with homework. Then, when I'm getting ready for school in the morning, I remember that I was supposed to read Chapter 22, or do problems 9-17. I always wonder, <u>Who</u> is that guy who keeps doing this to me?

20 No.

But I could never make myself tell Evan about my superstardom in the minors. Well, I almost did, once. A few days after Sara invited us to her party, I was over at Evan's house. We weren't playing video games or looking for music online or doing Facebook, or doing *anything*, because he was on Electronic Restriction. I didn't even ask him what for. His parents are so strict, it's ridiculous. He gets no warnings or anything. He'll be giving his little sister a hard time about something, nothing serious, then bang!—Electronic Restriction, just like that.[21] His room always has to be perfectly neat. Even his closet. It looks like something the aliens on whatever planet Sara finally decided I was from would have in one of their museums, on display behind an alien rope. SLEEPING AREA OF TYPICAL EARTH BOY, the sign would say.[22]

---

21 That's incredibly unfair because he's nice to her most of the time. Once I went over when the two of them were playing Parcheesi, and instead of taking off with me, he sat there and finished the game. I noticed that he kept passing up chances to catch one of her camels and send it all the way back. Instead he'd pretend he didn't see it, and move one of his other elephants. I know he was pretending because he's never missed a chance to send back one of my llamas.

22 No way would they use my room for a model. My parents gave up on it a long time ago. "Just don't take any food in there," my mom finally said. "We don't want to attract hyenas." I told her that hyenas aren't just scavengers, they sometimes hunt and kill their prey just like lions do. "That's why we don't want them in the house," she said.

So Evan and I started talking about who else we thought got invited to Sara's party, and whether or not there'd be dancing.

"*Yeah*, there's gonna be dancing," he said. "What else are we going to do, play Pin the Tail on the Donkey?"

"I can just see us all playing Duck Duck Goose," I said. "Or Musical Chairs."

"Musical Chairs, but with Coldplay or OutKast!" Evan yelled, jabbing his finger at me over and over, which he does when he gets really excited about some brilliant idea we've come up with. He started pacing back and forth. "Musical Chairs. That could actually work. Let's text Sara." I wasn't so sure about it, but Evan was already looking around for his phone.

"It's going to be weird no matter what," I said, "because you know there are going to be, like, thirty-five parents hanging around the house."

"And they'll be spying on us every five minutes," Evan said, opening and closing drawers in his desk. He started talking in this high-pitched voice he uses when he's imitating somebody's mother. "'Oh, look! Isn't that just too cute? Who's got a camera?'"

"It was a lot easier just doing little-kid stuff," I said. "Like when we used to go over to the park and play that Spaceman game just about every day."

Evan stopped all of a sudden. "Oh. Wait a minute." He slammed a drawer shut and sat down on the bed. "I forgot. Electronic Restriction." That meant his phone was in his mother's purse. No landline calls allowed either.[23]

An idea popped into my head, and I just blurted

---

23 My phone was at home. In my room. But I knew I'd find it somedt

it out. "Let's go to the park right now. We could play Spaceman one last time. You know—pretend to be little kids who don't have to worry about parties and pre-algebra and junk like that." Evan was jabbing his finger at me before I was even through talking. On our way out the door he turned around, went back to his bed, and smoothed out the bedspread.

We were lucky because nobody was anywhere near the monkey bars, which had always been our spaceship. From there we used to journey out into alien worlds (the kindergarten playground), then be taken captive aboard alien ships (the merry-go-round) and make daring escapes through wrecked civilizations (the seesaws).[24][25]

---

24 You can be just standing there, and if somebody pushes down on the other end of a seesaw, it can come up and bash you under the chin and make you almost bite your tongue in half. Or the guy riding on the other end can jump off and you come down so hard on your butt that your mouth snaps shut and you almost bite your tongue in half again a few months later. "If you only want half a tongue," my dad said after Seesaw Attack #2, "we can have a doctor do it, and not ruin any more T-shirts."

25 One thing about my dad is that he lies about almost everything. Not lies, really, but he hardly ever says anything normal. Like, if I walk into the kitchen and ask what's for dinner, he might say "mongoose" or "jackal." If he's giving my friends and me a ride somewhere, he'll all of a sudden say something like, "We've got a full tank of gas and a credit card. How about if we keep driving till we get to Las Vegas? It'll take the cops weeks to find us." My friends will say, "Las Vegas! Yeah!" They think he's hilarious. But I get pretty tired of it.

Evan climbed almost to the top and leaned out, holding on to a bar with one hand. As I was pulling myself up, he looked down and said, "What happened to your arm?"

"McNaught pushed me into a locker."

"Why does he hate you so much?"

"Because he's a jerk."

I should have used my other answer, because mentioning McNaught made things kind of awkward. Evan and McNaught aren't friends, exactly, but they both made the Little League All-Star team. Evan probably thought I'd been embarrassed about playing in the minors. So now seemed like a good time to tell him all about it.

But I didn't say anything, even though Evan's been my best friend since the second day of kindergarten, when a kid took away my dump-truck jigsaw puzzle, and Evan made him give it back.[26] If I started bragging about how great I was in the minors, it'd be like saying that I wasn't really good enough to keep up with him. That I was a level below him. And McNaught.

Well, I obviously was, in sports. But it was getting to seem like I was a level below him in everything else, too. Like, height. Evan's always been taller than me, but now he's *a lot* taller. And he's really popular. I'm not *un*popular, but I can tell that most people think of me as the guy who hangs out with Evan. Half the stuff I go to, I only find out about because of Evan, and then I end up going with him.

---

26 Todd Knoppsnyder. Then in fourth grade Knoppsnyder burped in my face, right after lunch on Enchilada Wednesday.

Anyway,[27] we climbed around on the monkey
bars for a few minutes without saying anything. I was
waiting for him to start playing Spaceman, and I guess
he was waiting for me. Once I thought about yelling,
"Look out!" and pulling out my beam gun and blasting the creature that had snuck up behind him, but I
looked around and saw some older guys walking by,
bouncing a basketball around, and two mothers pushing strollers. Evan was looking at them too.

When we played Spaceman before, it didn't matter
that the whole world could see us running around like
little morons, pretending monsters were after us. Now
it seems like all I do is worry about what people think
about me. The first time it really bothered me was about
a year ago, when I spent the night at Aaron Krugman's
house. We started acting really stupid. Aaron had a bag
of giant marshmallows, and we pretended they were
hand grenades. We tossed them all over his room. Then
we decided they were dinosaur eggs, and in no time at
all we had to shoot a whole lot of dinosaurs.

The next morning, while we were in the kitchen
eating breakfast,[28] Aaron's mother[29] asked us what

27 See what I mean about the "Anyways"?

28 When you stay over at somebody's house, you notice how
strange everything is. You expect the bed to be different, but then
the bedroom at night isn't quite as dark as your room, or maybe
it's darker. At breakfast you pick up a spoon, and it looks and
feels funny. The juice glasses are heavier. Or lighter, whatever. And
they don't have the same cereal. Or cereal bowls. It's just strange

29 Amazingly, there are even different parents at someone else's house

we'd been doing last night, and he *told* her: "We pretended the marshmallows were hand grenades, and then they were dinosaur eggs . . ."

He went on and on, describing everything we did. I couldn't believe it. She was only halfway paying attention, fooling around with the coffeemaker and saying, "Mmm-hmmm, oh, that's interesting, mmm-hmmm," but I wanted to kill Aaron anyway. I couldn't stop staring at him. He's such a baby, I suddenly realized. Our birthdays are only a few days apart, but I felt about twenty years older than him. He goes to another school now, and I haven't seen him since that morning.[30]

Evan and I never did get around to Spaceman. "I don't think we could play that stupid game even if we were positive no one would see us," he finally said. "Besides, we stopped because it got so boring. The last fifty times, all you did was yell that there was some creature sneaking up behind me, and blast it with your beam gun."

HO-O-O-O-O-O-N-N-K! A huge truck honked at us, my mind snapped back, and I was in the car, the city was way behind us, and we had been driving for—how long?

"About an hour," my mom said. I was in the backseat, right behind her. She tilted her head back to look at me. "Want something to snack on?"

"I'll wait," I said, and went back to figuring out who I wanted to be.

What was I like when I was the star pitcher? Well, I was really, really relaxed. Usually I talk fast, and try to get in what I want to say before somebody else says something.

---

30 My mom: "What ever happened to Aaron?" Me: "I dunno."

But with those younger guys on the team, I talked a little slower, because I knew they wouldn't interrupt me. My attitude was, I'm Number One, and I know it.

But I was still a pretty good guy. I never trashed any of those kids, or pushed anybody around. Not that I wanted to. But did I have to be so *nice* all the time?

Okay, so one thing different about Max at Camp would be that he'd act like he's Number One. And he wouldn't be so sickeningly nice.

If I could do it. If I could actually make myself into a different person.

"Look at that." My mom was pointing at a hand-painted sign taped to an overpass. "There's a crafts fair in that little town we're coming to. I'd really like to take a look." My dad didn't say anything. He hates going to these things as much as I do, and sometimes if he doesn't answer and just keeps on driving, that's the end of it.

But here was a chance to try doing something un–Max-like. I told myself, *One, two, three, GO!*

"Yeah, Dad," I said. "A crafts fair could be cool."

There was a long silence.[31] "All right," my dad finally said. He flipped on the turn blinker and started moving the car to the right lane. "Apparently, the voting patterns in this car have shifted." They were both so in shock that when we got to the crafts fair,[32] they let me get a chocolate shake, even though it was almost lunchtime.

The new Max was off to a good start.

---

31 Look at a clock for ten seconds. That's how long parents are in shock when you say something you'd never, ever, __ever__ say.

32 Boring.

chapter

WINDOW DRESSING;
SECRET ROOM;
BOXERS OR BRIEFS?

We were going past an incredibly smelly hog farm when I figured out that the only things people at camp would know about me would be whatever I *told* them. I'd been concentrating on how to act. But if I wanted to, I could say that I had a hot girlfriend, or that I was a surfer,[33] or that I work in a skateboard shop.

One thing I wouldn't be telling anybody is that I work in my parents' store. I don't exactly *have* to, but last year they told me that earning my allowance would mean helping out at the store sometimes, like Ben used to do.

"It'll be more money, sweetie," my mom said.[34]

---

33 I've tried surfing a couple of times. What most people don't know about it is that it's <u>hard</u>.

34 She doesn't call me "sweetie" in front of my friends anymore. And I only had to ask her not to 394 times.

"And it'll be good experience," my dad said, "in case you want to go into the business someday. You never know."

The only way I'm going to go into that business is after I've been turned down for every other job on earth, and if the planet that Sara thinks I'm from isn't hiring humans.

It isn't just that I don't really like working in a store. It's that our family business is *shmattes*, which is a Yiddish word that means "rags." Well, it kind of means "rags," but when you're talking about a business, it means clothes. In this case, women's clothes.

That's right. I work in a women's clothing store.

I empty wastebaskets and vacuum and Windex the mirrors—things like that. It's better when I work in the back room, out of sight. When boxes arrive from UPS, I unpack the new clothes and hang them up and enter their codes into a computer, which prints out tags with our store's name on it, and the price. Then I attach the tags to the sleeves, or whatever, with those thin little plastic strips.[35]

But Saturday morning is when my mom changes the window display. That means I have to climb into the front windows, the ones you look at as you walk by the store, and hand her clothes as she dresses and undresses all the mannequins. I'm obsessed with the idea that somebody I know is going to pass by and see me in the window with a bunch of naked women.

---

35 Everybody hates those things, and I'm one of the guys that puts them on stuff. Sorry.

22

Well, they're not really naked women.[36] But still, this is not something I want the whole world talking about. I try to get my mom to start as early as possible, so we can finish before the mall opens for customers.

"What's the big deal?" she asked me one time. "So somebody sees you with a mannequin. So what?"

So what? *So what?* So *nothing*, Mom. Hey, I've got an idea. Let's take one of these cool designer sweatshirts we sell AND MAKE IT INTO A BAG I CAN WEAR OVER MY HEAD FOR THE REST OF MY LIFE.

The new me, Max at Camp, does *not* work in a women's clothing store.

And I had to make sure, right away, that nobody thought they could push me around. I didn't want to get into a fight or anything, but I guessed I would if I had to. One thing I definitely didn't want was to go

---

36 There actually is one fun part about the mannequins. When they get worn-out-looking, my parents bring them home and put them in the garage until they can find somebody to buy them. Sometimes there are three or four of them out there. Without clothes, of course. When a friend comes over for the first time, I say, "Hey, you want to play Ping-Pong?" He says, "Sure," and I tell him the table's in the garage. We go out to the side door, and I say, "Go on in. I'll get the light." He takes a step or two inside, and I reach in and flick the switch. Do you know what a twelve-year-old guy does when he suddenly finds himself in a room full of naked women? I'll tell you what he does. He screams—and jumps about eight feet in the air.

around being afraid of someone, the way I was afraid of McNaught. He's the guy who hates me for no reason. Well, he started out hating me for no reason, but he's been such a jerk that lately I've been giving him reasons to.

Like what I did to him the Saturday after Sara invited me to her party. I was in the store's front window with my mom, really nervous because we got a late start and there were already people walking by. The job was taking extra long because I kept thinking I saw somebody I knew. When that happens, I step back, push open a door, and slip into a little secret room built into the wall, where we keep extra wigs and mannequin body parts. You can't even tell the door is there if you don't know where to look. Then I peek out through a crack in the doorway until the coast is clear.

But this time I was right. Who comes walking by? McNaught. I didn't even have time to think about what a close call that had been, because I noticed he wasn't alone. There was a woman with him. She looked like she was probably his mother. They were heading toward Macy's. McNaught was walking a couple of steps behind her and glancing around like he really didn't want anybody to see him.

When they were safely past the window, I jumped out of the secret room and actually helped my mom dress the last mannequin. We did it in record time. Then I said, "I'm going out for few minutes," and dashed for the front door before she finished saying the *N* in what I knew would be "No, you're not."

McNaught and his mother were already out of sight, but I was pretty sure they were in Macy's. Where else would they be—the video arcade? Victoria's Secret? I don't think so. I walked as fast as I could without looking like an idiot.

And I took the direct, public way, past all the other stores.

You know that secret room in our front window? Well, there are also hidden passageways behind the stores. They run the whole length of the mall on both sides. Delivery companies use them to get to the stores' back doors and deliver the tons and tons of junk that people come to the mall to buy.

There are even some unmarked doors in the mall leading to those passageways. You need a key to open them, but guess whose family owns one of the stores? And guess who found an extra key?

It takes longer, but that's how I like to get from one place to another in the mall. I slip through a secret door here, then reappear, like magic, way down there! I knew about the passageways because that's how deliveries come to our store, but Ben took me all through them one time.[37] It's like a mysterious, science-fiction world back there: long, long hallways, plain white walls, doors leading to all the different stores,

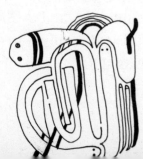

[37] Most of the time Ben thinks of me as a bug, but every now and then he'll act all big-brothery and let me in on some special knowledge he's picked up from living on earth so much longer than me.

a weird humming sound, hardly anybody around.[38]

Anyway, this time I took the regular way to Macy's because I wanted to get there fast. Macy's is a huge store, but it wasn't busy this early, so I was sure I could find McNaught and his mother. I worked out an escape route and tried not to worry about the consequences. McNaught would get me back, that was for sure. Probably it'd be worse than pushing me into a locker.[39] But it would be worth it.

I found them in Boys' Underwear, which was perfect. They were standing in front of a display wall stuffed with packs of briefs. I stayed a little ways away because I didn't want him to see me yet. I couldn't hear what his mother was saying, but she was holding two or three packs and trying to show them to him. He was looking away, hands jammed in his pockets.

I raced over to a rack of very cool-looking jackets,

---

38 Sometimes when I'm walking down one of those passageways, I pretend I'm in a wormhole, and each door leads to an alternate universe. I got the idea from my dad. One time, just for fun, I went out the side exit of a theater after we'd seen a movie. As I was going out, my dad said, in a loud voice, "Max, no! It's a wormhole! We might never get back to our own universe!" I whispered, "Dad, cut it out!" And he did, till we got to the car and he said, "I sure hope this universe has the same traffic rules that ours does." Now after every movie we go to, he wants to leave through a side exit. "Maybe this one will transport us back home again," he says. If I ignore him, he'll eventually stop. But he hasn't yet.

39 It was. Just wait.

pulled a bright red one off a hanger, and headed back. Mrs. McNaught was still holding the packs of underwear, and it sounded like she was getting mad.

"Or do you want boxers?" I heard her say as I got nearer. "Wiley, we are going to get you some underwear today, so you're just going to have to cooperate. The sooner we get it done . . ."

If McNaught hadn't already stopped listening to her, he sure stopped when he saw me coming.

I pretended like I didn't see him. No, I was just shopping, *on my own*, for a new jacket, holding it in one hand and looking around for a mirror so that I could check myself out. I walked just kind of toward them, which I knew would give McNaught hope that he might escape. But then—bad luck!—I turned my head, and what do you know? It's Wiley McNaught!

"Hey, Wiley," I said, all casual and friendly. "What are you doing here?"

No answer. I acted like I didn't notice. "I'm thinking about getting this jacket, but I dunno. Gotta find a mirror."

He slumped farther into the My Mother's Giving Me a Lecture position.[40] Mrs. McNaught was holding the packs of underwear practically right under his nose.

"Underwear!" I said. "Good idea. Hey, is that for Sara's party? She'll appreciate that. I'll text her about how I saw you here buying underwear with your mother."

---

40 There's a drawing of the correct My Mother's Giving Me a Lecture position on page 108 of <u>How to Drive Your Parents Insane</u>. That's the book that the government mails to kids when they turn eleven. You got one, right?

Mrs. McNaught stood there half smiling. No idea what was going on. None.

"Well, I gotta take off," I said. "See you around." I looked up at his mother and smiled. "Bye, Mrs. McNaught." I'm *such* a polite boy.

As I walked away, I heard McNaught saying, "These are fine, these are fine, whatever," and I knew I had to hurry. I tossed the jacket onto a sale table and looked over my shoulder and yup, here he comes. He wasn't headed straight for me, because he had to weave around some racks of clothes, but he was going to be here real soon. He couldn't just start hitting me in public, but there are all kinds of things that people like McNaught can do to hurt you without attracting attention.

The race was to see if I could get out of Macy's far enough in front of him. Then I could run, and all I needed was a decent head start. I pushed open the door and took off. The first store on the left is Radio Shack, and next to it there's a plain, locked door that nobody ever notices.

I didn't either till Ben showed it to me.

What happened next I can't say, because I didn't see it. But it probably looked like this: McNaught came out of Macy's and started running after me. Then he stopped. And looked around. And looked around some more. There was only one place I could have gone: Radio Shack. So he went inside. Radio Shack isn't a very big store. It didn't take him long to figure out I wasn't there. I had vanished into thin mall air.

So he went back into Macy's, where his mother was

still holding those packs of underwear. And she said . . . well, you can make up that part as easily as I can.

But I can tell you exactly what *my* mother was saying at about the same time, as I came in the back door of the store from the hallway used by delivery guys and me. She was saying, "That was quick."

"I saw a guy from school and needed to talk to him, is all," I said. "You want me to put price tags on these belts?"

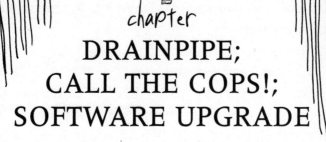

chapter 4
DRAINPIPE;
CALL THE COPS!;
SOFTWARE UPGRADE

We didn't stay at the crafts fair very long because my dad and I shifted into what my mom calls our Stunned Oxen mode. That's when we follow her around and just stand there with blank looks on our faces while she shops.

"Okay, Stunned Oxen, that's it, let's go," she said after going through a table piled with scarves that looked exactly like the scarves she goes through at every other crafts fair she's ever dragged us to. "You two look so miserable, I can't stand it anymore."

"What?" my dad said, like he didn't know what she was talking about. "No, go ahead, take as much time as you want."

"Yeah," I said. "We'll wait." [4]

---

4 Since I was playing a Stunned Ox, I said it with a completely flat voice.

"Nope, we're outta here." She was already walking toward the car. "I don't know why I bother.[42] But you owe me. I get to pick where we stop for lunch."

"Deal!" my dad and I said together. My mom looked back and laughed.

"You guys," she said.

"Us guys," my dad said.

I can tell that he really likes it when we work together like that, teaming up against my mom.[43] And since he was treating me like an equal, it was a good time to bring up something that they'd been saying "no" to. My mom was walking up ahead a little ways, which made us even more buddy-buddy.

"Hey," I said, "have you thought any more about me having my own room at the motel[44] tonight?" We wouldn't be getting to the camp until the next day.

---

42 Neither do I. My dad and I are really good at being Stunned.

43 Sometimes I do the same thing with her against him. "You have to remember that your father's an odd duck," she says when we're planning something sneaky. I guess that's when he's not busy being a Stunned Ox.

44 I like just about everything about motels, except that when I was little, I had to share a bed with Ben because my parents would just get one room, with two queen beds. Now we get our own room, with our own beds. We talk and goof around. He always lets me be the one to go down the hall to the ice machine to fill up the little plastic bucket with ice. We never use any of it, but we get a bucket of ice anyway, because that's what you're supposed to do when you're in a motel.

"Max, we already explained that we're not going to pay for two rooms if we don't have to." He was back to talking like a parent again. "You'll have a bed all to yourself. So I don't want to hear—"

"Come on, Dad." I tried to make my voice not sound whiny, but that's the way it was coming out. "It's creepy to share a motel room with you guys. And we're already going to be sharing a stupid cabin all week, so—"

"No," he said, and started walking faster. When he caught up with my mom, he leaned his head toward her, and I knew he was saying that Max was being a pain in the butt about the motel again, and that she was telling him to just ignore me.

Okay, so I just figured out another thing I was going to do—I mean, not do—at camp: hang around with *them*.

When we got back to the car, I told myself not to slam the door, but after I got in, something took over my body and made me slam it anyway. My dad was putting on his seat belt, and he turned around to say something that was for sure going to be about tantrums and acting my age, but my mom shot over a just-keep-ignoring-him look.

What I really hate is when they treat me like I'm a little kid, and then I get so mad that I actually start *acting* like one. Like slamming the car door. I had no control—I just sort of watched myself do it.

Of course, when I was younger, I didn't even think about trying not to do dumb things. I just went ahead and did them. They didn't seem that way when I started out, because who *wants* to do something dumb? But by the end it was pretty obvious. Then I'd wonder: When am I going to be able to realize something's dumb before I actually do it?

Here's a perfect example. There's a drain in our street, built into the side of the sidewalk down at the end of the block. When we play Wiffle ball in the Crenshaws' huge yard across the street, we have to put some cardboard boxes in front of the drain, because it's just big enough for a Wiffle ball to go through. We must have lost 640 of them that way.[45]

One day a couple of summers ago I was messing around with some kids in my neighborhood. We were in an empty lot that was down a gully and about a hundred yards away from the drain. Somebody said, "Look! A drainpipe!" The end of a huge pipe was sticking out of the side of the hill. I'd known it was there for a long time, but never paid any attention to it. There was a metal screen to keep animals and really stupid

_____

45   If I had said, "We must have lost four or five," it would have been the truth, but it would have been kind of dull. So writing "640 Wiffle balls" isn't lying, it's just exaggerating for fun. And for some reason, when you exaggerate that way, it helps to pick a really big number. If I'd said, "We must have lost eight of them," it wouldn't be funny. In fact, you'd probably think, "What a bunch of idiots! Why didn't they put something in front of the drain sooner?" Same with "We must have lost twelve of them that way." But "We must have lost thirty-seven of them that way" is starting to get interesting, because it's starting to sound ridiculous. Now, 640—that's really ridiculous.

kids out, but it had come loose and was just sort of hanging there.

"I bet this is where the drain in the street leads to," I said.

"Let's find out," said a kid named Gabe, who's a year older than me, and always just goes ahead and *does* things. The pipe was just big enough to crawl into. He pushed the screen aside, and in he went. With me right behind him. Don't ask me why. I just felt like I had to.

It was *so* dark and strange in there.[46] The very bottom of the pipe was mud, and there were cobwebs, and moldy and rotten stuff that I couldn't see very well but didn't want to think about anyway. It smelled weird— wet and stale at the same time. We were crawling on our knees and elbows, getting really filthy, but there was light up ahead that we were sure was coming from the drain in the street. I was kind of sorry I was doing this, but I could hear the other kids' shouts echoing through the pipe. And Gabe's sneakers, right in front of me, kept scooting forward. So I did too.

It took us about ten minutes to get to the end,[47]

---

46 Alice would never have gone in. She's got too much sense.

47 I first wrote "twenty minutes," even though I knew it was actually about ten. This is a different kind of exaggeration, where people make things bigger or faster or scarier, or whatever, when they tell about something they saw or something that happened to them. It's hard not to. You just do it automatically, for some reason. My dad says that he always assumes other people are exaggerating,

go to next page

where there was a short, wide chamber going up. At the top of that, just a couple of feet above us, light poured through the opening that had been the Wiffle ball black hole. We were there. So were all the other kids, jumping around in the street, laughing and yelling. They made so much noise that Mrs. Crenshaw came out of her house to see what was going on.

We saw her legs coming toward us as she crossed the street, then just her sandals and ankles. She bent down, and there was her big red face, right in front of us. She gasped. "What in the world?!" Then she said, "Gabriel! And who is that behind you—Max? You boys come out of there right now!"

"Okay, okay," Gabe said. We started trying to turn around, but there was no room. We'd have to crawl back backward, which would be harder and slower.

"Right now!" Mrs. Crenshaw was yelling. "You come out right now!"

I'd already started back. It was harder and slower, all right.

so in his mind he reduces whatever numbers they say by about 25 percent. He says that he exaggerates too, because he's sure they think he's exaggerating, so if he _doesn't_ exaggerate, they'll think the real numbers he's saying are exaggerations, and make them smaller in _their_ minds. That means that the only way to get to the truth is to lie. So everybody's lying to everybody else, except they all know about the lies, and in the end everybody is able to figure out what the truth is. I asked my dad why they aren't just honest to begin with, and he said he's asked himself that same question seven thousand times.

"We have to go back the way we came," Gabe called to her. "We'll be out in a few minutes."

"You come out right now," Mrs. Crenshaw yelled again, "or I'm going to call your parents and tell them you're stuck!"

"WE'RE NOT STUCK!" Gabe and I screamed. "No! No! *DON'T CALL OUR PARENTS!*"

We were scrambling backward as fast as we could, knee-elbow-knee-elbow, knee-elbow-knee-elbow. Gabe's sneakers kept mashing into my face until finally he got me square in the nose. *Great,* I thought. *Blood.*

Mrs. Crenshaw did call. I heard all about it later. She really did say that we were stuck in a drainpipe.[48] But she didn't even wait to get my mom or dad on the phone. She just told the salesclerk who answered to tell them that their son Max was stuck in a drainpipe.[49]

"Little Max is stuck in a drainpipe!" the clerk screamed.[50]

A customer said, "What?"

Another customer said, "A little boy is stuck in a drainpipe!"

"Somebody call the police!"

"Somebody call the fire department!"

And somebody did.

---

48 Adults can be just as dumb as kids.

49 Even dumber.

50 See what I mean?

Gabe and I were walking back up toward the street when we heard a car screech to a stop. Two doors slammed, and there were my parents, looking down the gully at us. I yelled, "We weren't stuck—we *told* Mrs. Crenshaw not to call." My mother was crying. My father had one hand on her shoulder and the other hand on his head, like he was trying to keep his brains from blowing out the top.

Gabe changed direction and headed off to somewhere else.

"Oh, Max!" my mother said when I got up to the street. She had her arms open for a Big Hug, but when she got close, she changed her mind and took a couple of steps back.

I was covered with cobwebs and splattered with slime and mud. There was blood on my face and the front of my T-shirt. My dad turned and walked toward the police car and the fire truck that had just pulled up. "This way," he said to me.

The two policemen waved the fire truck away. Then, with their hands on their hips, they just stood there and stared at me for a minute.[51]

---

51 I exaggerated without even knowing it! It was nowhere near a minute. I know because I just followed the second hand of a clock while it went all the way around. If you try it, you'll see that a minute can be a real long time. My mom says that a lot of times "a minute" is just an expression, and no one really thinks you mean an exact minute, as in sixty seconds. So I wasn't exaggerating after all. Never mind.

"Son," said the taller one, the one without a mustache, "what you and your buddy did was . . ." Well, as best I can remember, it was dangerous, not smart, we nearly scared our poor parents to death, and they and the fire department got called out here when they could have been doing other, really important things, and they sure hoped we'd never do anything like that again. Some other stuff too, probably. It was hard to pay attention, because I kept thinking about how much trouble I was going to be in at home.

When the policeman was finished, my dad apologized, and told me to apologize. My mom had driven the car home, so we walked. It was only about a block, but it seemed a lot farther. I showered and put on clean clothes. My dad was sitting at the kitchen table, pretending to reread the paper he'd read that morning. I sat down and waited.

My mother came in. We all sat there for a few minutes.[52] Finally my mom said, "Well, it's pretty late. There's no point in going back to the store."

"Max," my dad said, "set the table and start some water for pasta."

The next day, as my dad was putting clothes into the washing machine, he said, "What is it with you and bloody T-shirts?"

And that was it. No screaming, no How Could You Have Done Such a Thing?, no You Don't Have The

---

52 Real minutes.

Sense that God Gave Geese.[53] I kept worrying about what they were going to do to me, but they never did anything. They never even *said* anything.

That made me think about it even more. Finally, a few days later, I did this thing that I do when I realize something all of a sudden. I stop, hold myself perfectly still, and say it out loud. I was on my way to catch the bus to school when it came to me.

"They *want* me to keep thinking about it," I said. "They're trying to install 'This Is Dumb' software in my brain."

Then I walked on to the bus stop, maybe[54] just a little bit smarter than I was before. That's another way of saying, not quite as dumb.

---

53 One of my grandfather's favorite sayings.

54 I said, *maybe*.

chapter

CLOSET DOOR;
SAM GETS THE POINT;
BAD REPUTATION

W e'd hardly gotten back on the freeway before my mom started talking about where we should eat.[55] She absolutely will not, under any circumstances, no matter how hungry she is, *ever* go to a fast-food restaurant. That'd be okay, except that she also absolutely will not, under any circumstances, no matter how hungry *I* am, ever take *me* to a fast-food restaurant. When she hears that one of my friends' mom or dad has taken us someplace like McDonald's, she says, "What's the matter with those people?"

So we got right back *off* the freeway because she wanted to stay in the crafts-fair town and find "someplace local." That can mean driving around and

---

55 If you pay attention, you'll be amazed at how much time people spend on this subject.

around while my dad gets madder and madder, but at the bottom of the off-ramp, right across the street, there was a combination restaurant and grocery store. The sign said BALDAUF FARMS: FRESH FOOD, FRESH PRODUCE.

"Okay, you guys," she said, "tell me that doesn't look better than some fast-food joint."

I said, "That doesn't look better than some fast-food joint."

"You're not getting your own room, Max," my dad said. "Get over it."

"No," I said, but I kind of was already. I just had to keep it up for a while to make sure that they understood that it was important, that this wasn't about a little kid throwing a two-minute fit.[56] They should know by now how I feel about having my own space.

A couple of years ago I got really, really sick of sharing a room with Ben.[57] One night, lying in bed, I started thinking about the storeroom down the hall that my dad was always talking about turning into an office. I fantasized what it would be like to

---

56 Whenever somebody in preschool whined and cried because they didn't get exactly what they wanted, one of the teachers would say in this sing-songy voice, "You get what you get, and you don't throw a fit." Of the ten thousand annoying things stuck in my head that I'd like to get rid of, that's about number three.

57 It was like living in a cage with a grizzly bear—it did whatever it wanted, you had to stay out of its way, and every now and then it'd attack you and tear you to pieces.

have my own room, to be able to close a door and know I was going to be alone. I tried and tried to arrange the storeroom in my head, like I did with the suitcases for the car trunk that one time. Finally, around midnight, I got up and went to check it out. It seemed like it wasn't going to work because if I put in a bed, a desk, a chair, and a bookcase, there'd hardly be room to stand up. Then came the moment of genius: Take the sliding door off the big closet, and put the bed in there. If I hung a sheet or a bed-spread or something in front of it, I'd have an even *more* private space.

"Well, sure, why not?" my mom said at breakfast. I didn't even have to use any of the twenty-two reasons I had ready.

My dad said, "What about our office?"

"Oh, that's right. Max, your father's going to get up from the table right now and start converting the storeroom into an office."

They looked at each other. Then he looked at me and said, "Ben can help you."

Ben walked into the kitchen and said, "Help him what?" Five seconds later he said, "How about right after school today?" [58]

The bed fit into the closet with maybe two inches to spare on either side. A couple of feet above where my head was going to be, Ben put up a shelf big enough to

---

58 Even grizzly bears can cooperate if there's something in it for them.

hold a reading light and a book or two. Then he found some hooks and an old curtain, and hung it where the closet doors had been.

"This is looking pretty good," he said when we'd finished setting everything up. "Want to trade?"

"No, and get out of my room." I said it in a kidding voice, hoping to get away with it.

He laughed. "Not bad," he said. "Score one for you." And he left.[59]

Lunch at that Baldauf Farms place turned out okay because I got them to make a plain grilled-cheese sandwich, without any of the lettuce or tomato or horseradish or other junk that the menu said was in their Farm-Fresh Cheese Sandwich Deluxe. "No thanks, just cheese," I kept saying as the waiter kept asking, "But don't you want—?" When the sandwich finally came, it was just cheese. I checked.

Back on the road, I was sleepy from lunch and from getting up so early to help pack, and I drifted into doing something I hadn't done for a long time— pretending there's a beam gun mounted on the roof, and firing blaster rays at cars on the other side of the freeway. I vaporized a couple hundred of them, kind of laughing at myself because it's such a little-kid thing to do. *Man*, I thought, *if I told anybody about this, they'd probably send me to a child psychologist, and I'd have to convince him that I didn't really want to hurt anybody.*

59 Grizzly bears understand territory.

But I knew I didn't really want to hurt anybody because I'd done that already.

I twitched in my seat, the way you do when all of a sudden you remember something embarrassing that happened to you. And thinking about hurting people had reminded me of Sam.

Okay, this next part is going to sound pretty awful. But I learned something, and no, it wasn't that it's not good to hurt people. I knew that already.

One afternoon in fifth grade, we got called into an assembly. I can't remember what it was for.[60] We all filed in, class by class, and sat down. I had a pencil in my pocket, one I'd just sharpened. I took it out and smelled its fresh-wood smell, and touched my thumb to the point a few times. It was really, really sharp.

Sam Gellar was next to me. We're not good friends or anything, but he's okay. Both of his parents are doctors, and he lives in a huge house. A lot of kids think he's stuck-up, because he always has brand-name clothes and sneakers and stuff, but mostly he's just quiet and smart.

Anyway, Sam stood up for some reason, and I thought it'd be funny to hold my pencil on his chair, with its point up. The idea was, he'd see it, and we'd both laugh—*Ha, ha, wouldn't THAT hurt?*[61] I put the

---

60 I can't remember what most assemblies I've been to were for.

61 You don't have to tell me. I know how un-funny that sounds. But I was a fifth grader.

eraser end of the pencil on the chair and looked up to say, "Hey, Sam!"—but he was already on his way to sitting down.

You know how when people describe something horrible that happened to them, a lot of times they say, "It was like everything was in slow motion"? Well, it wasn't like that at all. It was incredibly fast: *pencil-look-up-WHUMP!* and he was on it. I heard a soft *pop!* as the pencil point punched through his jeans, and I could feel it sink into the left side of his butt.

He jumped up even faster. He gasped but didn't yell. He just grabbed his butt with his left hand and stood there for a few seconds with his eyes closed tight. When he opened them and started blinking, tears were pouring out.

"Sam, I'm sorry," I said. "I—" But he was already shuffling sideways down the row, on his way to the school nurse. I sat through the assembly, whatever it was, then went back to class and waited to get called to the principal's office.

I'm not going to tell you all the details about what happened next, because you can guess pretty well: Our parents got called, and I got detention. But eventually I got everybody to believe that I hadn't meant to hurt him, and that I would never, ever, *ever* again put a sharpened pencil under somebody's butt.[62]

---

62 If anybody asks you what this book is about, just say, "It's about how you're not supposed to put a sharpened pencil under somebody's butt." Don't use that in a book report, though.

Anyway, that whole thing got me started think-ing about something complicated. Something that I haven't quite figured out yet.

There are guys at school who like to go around hurting people—guys like McNaught. And McNaught isn't even that bad, compared to some of them. He just seems to like hurting *me*. And then there are guys like me, who don't do anything like that, who never pick on anybody. Yet in just a few stupid sec-onds, I went and hurt Sam probably worse than any of those bullies ever hurt anybody. And that's not even the most confusing part.

Because I got rewarded for it. A couple of months later I was riding my bike around the neighborhood next to ours. Three guys about a year older than me[63] were sitting on their bikes in a driveway. They ped-aled out into the street and stopped right in front of me. I had to stop too.

"Where do you think you're going?" one of them said.

I said, "I'm just riding around."

"What makes you think you can ride around here?" That was the same kid. He had short blond hair that stuck straight up, and a white T-shirt that was so dirty, I couldn't even read what was written on it.

---

63 My dad says that when you grow up, you lose the ability to look at somebody for less than a second and know if he's older, younger, or the same age as you. He also says that I won't be able to fall down stairs without breaking sixteen bones, or drink a "suicide"—that's when you fill your cup with every kind of soda in the machine—without throwing up.

"I don't know," I said. I admit this wasn't a great answer.

"Nice bike," Dirty T-Shirt said. "Maybe we're gonna—"

"Hey, Tyler," one of the other kids said. He pointed at me. "I think that's the guy . . ." He leaned over from his bike and whispered something.

"You stabbed somebody?" Dirty T-Shirt/Tyler said. "I don't believe it. No way."

"Okay," I said. "Go ahead and don't believe it."

"What a liar." But he began backing away on his bike. So did the other two. I put my foot on the pedal and gave it a big push.

"You better not come back around here," he said as I whooshed by him.

Once I got going fast, I yelled over my shoulder, "I'll go anywhere I want!" [64]

Why did I get away so easily? Because I'd hurt Sam. One of those guys must have heard about it, but by the time the story got to him, it had changed to something like, "You see that kid over there? He stabbed a guy," instead of "That's the moron who put a pencil under somebody's butt."

At the time, I didn't think too much about it. I was just glad I escaped. But lately it's been bothering me when people say, "Things happen for a reason." I've

---

[64] I really do go anywhere I want. It's just that I don't <u>want</u> to go down that street anymore.

tried to make it fit into the Sam/bicycle incident, but I can't. Sam got hurt so that those guys would think I was dangerous and crazy, and leave me alone? That doesn't make any sense to me.

But it's scary to believe that things happen for no reason at all. That means *anything* can happen. At any time.

And that got me thinking about Alice. About what I *did* to Alice. But it's not time for that story yet. I don't think you're ready to hear it, and I know I'm not ready to tell it.

My parents had loaded the car's CD player with their favorite stuff: really dull rock. After a while the road noise mixed in with the music, then faded away, then mixed with the music again, and then I was out.

chapter

SPF 30; TROUBLE
WITH AMOEBAS;
SPECIAL DELIVERY

The slam of the car door yanked me awake. "Hmmm?" I said, and looked around. Parking lot. "You had a good sleep." My mom had stayed in the car while my dad went . . . Where were we? Motel?

"We decided to stop a little early," my mom said. "There's plenty of time tomorrow, since we can't even check into the camp till after lunch. Right now we can just relax and go for a swim. If your father manages to get us a room, that is."

He did. We carried the things we needed for the night up to a second-floor room with a balcony overlooking the pool. I stood on the balcony, and two teenage girls were sunbathing right below me. One of them was in a lounge chair, reading a magazine. The other was lying facedown on a towel next to the pool, letting her right arm drift back and forth in the water. Their sunscreen hit me like an ocean wave. I sat down in a plastic Adirondack chair and put my feet up on the railing.

"Max, we're not through," my dad said from inside the room. We still had to bring up stuff that didn't fit in the trunk, so nobody'd rip it off. He stepped out onto the balcony and saw the two girls, and saw me looking at them. "Oh," he said.

I jumped out of the chair and said, "Come on." [65]

Instead of going back to the balcony after we moved everything in, I put on my swim trunks and went down to the pool. After my parents did, that is. As if I was going to walk down with them. I could just imagine those girls looking up, and here comes a family—the mother and the father and their little boy. Right.

I sat in a lounge chair opposite the girls, on the other side of the pool and far away from my mom and dad, and pulled a baseball cap down low. The book on my lap was in a perfect position for glancing over. The girls were a lot older than me, maybe fifteen or sixteen. They didn't know me, would *never* know me, and probably barely even knew I was there. But it was still important that they didn't think of me as a little kid. That was a feeling I never wanted to have again.

The thing is, I didn't even know that I felt like a little kid until I stopped feeling like one. Since then it's mostly been good. Mostly. But not all of it.

My absolute favorite time of the week used to be

65 It's just too weird when my dad notices me noticing girls.

Saturday morning. If everything went just right, I'd half wake up and lie in bed sort of thinking I had to get up to go to school. As I got more and more awake, I'd begin to realize that it was, like, eighty thirty, way past time for school, which meant that it must be—

I'd sit up in bed and say, "Saturday!" Then I'd let myself fall back down, and lie there thinking about what I wanted to do, or not do, all day. Sometimes I'd even go back to sleep for a while. The best part was the feeling that began in my chest, this rushing, excited *happiness* that would then wash over my whole body. Saturday!

Now, most days, I feel the exact opposite. I know I don't really hate school, or the teachers, or the people at school, or my parents, or anybody. But here's what it's like when I wake up. And not just on school days or days I have to work in the store:

I get out of bed and walk toward the bathroom, but it's more like I'm falling, and every step I take just keeps me from going face-first down onto the floor. When I get into the bathroom, I close the door, turn on the light, and fall over to the sink. I put my hands on the edge and just lean there for half a minute,[66] with my head hanging down. Then I look at myself in the mirror, and this dull awfulness sweeps over me.

---

66 Since I looked at the clock for a whole minute while I was writing Chapter 5, I've gotten pretty good at judging how long something takes. So I really do stand there like that for about thirty seconds.

It's not even caused by anything, like a test that day or homework I forgot about. It's just the way I *am*.

It gets better as the day goes on. A lot of times, the feeling goes away completely. But it's always pretty bad at breakfast. My dad makes it worse, because he's the kind of person who likes to say "Good morning!" and I'm not. He mentioned my "moodiness" to the doctor the last time I had a checkup. The doctor asked me a few questions, then said that all this was probably caused by hormones. I really, really didn't want to get into that. So I told him I didn't feel all that bad, and he talked for a little bit about how what I was feeling was perfectly normal, and I said I know, and he said to be sure to tell my parents if it got worse, and I said I would. I managed to get the conversation over with in about two minutes,[67] which was about all I could stand.

The girl with the magazine caught me staring. I quickly looked down at my book, but felt like an idiot and looked back up again. She might have smiled a little—it was hard to tell. Anyway, she went back to her magazine. I pretended to read the book, but really I was wondering if there'd ever be a time when I'd be able to just smile at a girl, or at least smile back, even walk around the pool and sit down and start talking. Well, the camp would be a good place to practice. The new Max was going to spend some time hanging out with girls. He was going to be unpredictable and interesting. I hoped.

---

67 Maybe you should sit by a clock while you read this book.

The old Max sure wasn't. Except with Allie Fowler. And at first not even with her.

Earlier this year, back in seventh grade, right after winter break, our science teacher, Ms. O'Connor, picked Allie and me to do a special project,[68] because we're both pretty good in science. It was about amoebas, these animals that are so small, you need a microscope to see them. So Ms. O set us up with a microscope in the room behind the main science room. The first time Allie and I came out to ask a question, people went, "OOOOOOoooooo! Max and Allie! OOOOOOooooooo!"

Ms. O said, *"Hey!"* and they all shut up because she's a great person and nobody wants her to be mad at them. But after she answered our question and we turned to go back into the room, I saw that Allie was really upset. So I went to my desk and pretended to look for something, and basically stalled until class was over.

The amoeba project took all week, and I felt awkward from the start. All I could think about was that I was in this small room with Allie. She and Sara are good friends, but I'd never paid much attention to Allie because she's so quiet. Shy, I guess. Around boys, anyway. She has reddish-brown hair and nearly invisible glasses, the kind without any rims. When she's standing right next to you, she tilts her head forward and looks at you over the top of those

---

68 For extra credit, of course. I asked.

glasses. I kept noticing that her eyes are dark brown, but incredibly bright.

It made me almost useless on the project, because I was mostly concentrating on stuff I could say to make her think I was cool, which was hard because I was feeling like such a geek. I guess I was also concentrating on not saying anything that would make her think I was a geek, which is just as hard. I spent the first few days just feeling bad.

But everything turned out all right. I mean, it turned out *good*. By the end of the week it was starting to feel natural to be around her, and I was pretty much able to be myself. I hoped that was okay, because, obviously, I spend a lot of time wishing I could be a lot different from what I am. More like Evan, for example. He just stands around and talks to girls, or texts three or four of them practically at the same time. Sometimes I just stare at him doing it.

And I didn't think about it at the time, but it must have gotten easier for Allie, too, because by the time we were finished, she sure wasn't quiet or shy around *me*.

When we turned in the amoeba project, Ms. O reached under her desk and pulled out a huge book. "It's a catalog of scientific equipment," she said. "I use it to order stuff. For some reason the company sent me an extra one. Do you guys want it?"

Did we want it? *Yeah*, we wanted it.

"You take it first," Allie said after class.

"No, you," I said.

"No, you," she said.

There's only one way to end an argument like that: "One, two, *three!*"

She papered my rock, and told me to take the catalog home. I said okay, but that I'd bring it back the next day.

After dinner I flipped through it. All kinds of great stuff was in there. But looking at pictures of scientific equipment gets pretty boring pretty fast. I decided that when Allie said it was my turn to have it again, I'd tell her she could keep it.

"Here you go," I said as I handed her the catalog in Ms. O's class the next day. Allie was *so* happy I'd remembered to bring it in.

"Here you go," she said in Ms. O's class the day after that, as she plopped the catalog on my desk.

"Oh, that's okay," I said. "I don't need to look at it anymore."

"It's your turn to have it," she said. "And you can keep it as long as you want."

"Okay," I said. I picked up the catalog and held it out to her. "I choose to keep it for five seconds."

She put her hands behind her back. "Oh no," she said. "You have to keep it until tomorrow. Those are the rules."

I said, "What rules?"

"Well . . . the Scientific Catalog-Keeping Rules. The other guy has to hold on to it for at least a day."

"What if I just throw it away?"

Allie pretended to be shocked. "You better not!" she

said. "That's *really* against the rules. Besides, it's half mine. You can't throw away somebody else's stuff." She turned around and walked to her desk.

The next day was Friday. When I got to school, I gave the catalog to Evan. Later, when Allie came in to science class, she looked at my desk, then looked at my backpack.[69] She was trying to see if there was something big and heavy in there.

I shrugged. "Forgot."

She smiled. "Too bad."

On the way out of class, Evan took the catalog out of *his* backpack and passed it to me. Allie was walking up ahead. I hurried until I was right behind her. "Hey, Allie!" I said. She stopped and turned around. "I hope lying isn't against the rules, because I didn't really forget." I handed her the catalog. "Have a good weekend," I said, and walked away.

Sunday morning my mother said, "Someone left something for you. It was leaning against the front door." She handed me a package wrapped in brown paper. "For Max" was written on it. And below that, in big red letters, "SPECIAL DELIVERY."

"Aren't you going to open it?" she asked.

But I got Allie back right away. I used Sara, because even though everybody *says* they can keep a secret,

---

[69] My backpack is blue. That's *not important*, but footnotes are very sensitive, and they get their feelings hurt if you go too long without using them.

Sara really can.[70] And the truth is, she not only helped me out, she came up with the whole plan.

"I'm going to Allie's house Saturday night," she said. "We're going to watch movies and eat about seventeen bowls of popcorn. I'll put it in a plastic bag. It's perfect."

"Okay," Allie said in school a couple of weeks later, "how did that catalog get into the back of our freezer?"

"What catalog?" I said. "Oh, *that* catalog. Do you have it? I lost track. Why don't you just keep it?"

"I will," she said. "For now."

Scientists say there's no such thing as ESP, but I still tried to send a message to the girl in the chair on the other side of the pool: *You're not cold. Don't put on your T-shirt.* It was late afternoon, and I'd been watching the motel's shadow move slowly across her body. Less than a minute after my ESP attempt, she reached into a big straw handbag, pulled out a tie-dyed T-shirt, and put it on. Maybe she misheard me.

---

70 Trying to keep a secret is another example of being different people at different times. When somebody asks me if I can keep a secret, I always say yes, and I always mean it. But sometimes I go and tell it anyway. That is, the Other Me tells. It sure wasn't the Me who promised not to, because he wasn't lying. My mom says that when you find yourself about to tell a secret, you should concentrate on keeping your mouth closed. She also says that there are a lot of other times when keeping your mouth closed is the best thing you can possibly do. I asked her how to know when it's one of those times, and she said she's still trying to learn that herself.

chapter

CUTE STUFF; OH NO; TRANSPORTER MALFUNCTION

It was bad enough that I didn't get my own room at the motel. Now, instead of two queen beds, there was a queen bed and a little couch that folded out into a single bed. Actually, it was pretty comfortable, but since my mom was being really apologetic about it, I acted like it wasn't. "But that's okay," I said, all grown-up–like. "It's just one night." Maybe this would get me my own room on the trip back.

When we turned off the lights, I was still wide-awake, probably because I'd slept so long in the car, so I went back to work on my New Max project. By this time tomorrow, I said to myself, I'll have been at the camp for half a day. If I just sort of watch other people to see what's happening, groups will form and I'll be out before I start. Besides, I didn't want the New Max to wait for things to happen—I wanted him to make things happen. Somehow I was going to force myself to act, to just go ahead and *do stuff*.

I pictured myself at camp—and then I realized what was wrong with the picture.

It didn't take me half a minute to come up with my new look. Not only would it make me supercool, but I knew it'd make me feel different too. Almost like wearing a costume, except it really would be me. The New Max.

A *snort!* came from the queen bed. That was my dad. I waited for him to start snoring, but he didn't. Every now and then I could hear a car pulling into or out of the motel parking lot. I turned over again, and stared at the dark shape of the minifridge about three feet away. The hum eventually put me to sleep.

And it was the hum of the minifridge that woke me up. At least, that's the only sound I could hear except for my parents' breathing, and I had to concentrate to hear that. No clock was in sight, but there was soft light behind the curtains in front of the sliding door to the balcony. I couldn't remember if the light had been there before, coming from some outdoor motel light, or if it was actually getting to be morning. I hoped it meant morning, because this was one of those times when you open your eyes and *bam!*, you're wide-awake, right now. That's okay if it's close to time to get up, but not so okay if it turns out to be, like, three thirty.

Anyway, I wasn't going back to sleep, no matter what time it was, because this was the day I was going to stop being Max. *Well,* I thought, *I'll still be Max, but*

I'll be more than Max. I'll be Max Plus. Extra-Strength Max. Uber-Max. Max with Enhanced Memory. Max with Added Levels of Difficulty. Max with a Special Features DVD. Max—

"Max?" my mom whispered, "Are you awake?"

"Yeah."

"I can't sleep either. Let's go down to the coffee shop."

We got up and got dressed, and made it out the door to the outside walkway without waking up my dad. It *was* getting light out, but since this was the middle of summer, it was still pretty early—5:40, said a clock in the motel's coffee shop. My dad would want a big breakfast when he got up, so we just ordered coffee and orange juice.

"Coffee's starting to smell good to me," I said to my mom when the waitress set a big white mug in front of her. I picked it up, took a whiff, and tried a sip. "Still tastes horrible, though."

"You're going to be a coffee drinker," she said. "It's obvious. Ben still won't touch it. It beats me how he's getting through college."

I liked it that my mom said I was going to be a coffee drinker. She was imagining me grown up. I also liked it that we were there together in the already-busy coffee shop so early in the morning, hundreds of miles from home, with strangers all around us, and the smell of toast and bacon and coffee, and dishes clanking, and trucks and cars moving around in the big parking lot. Two travelers.

"So," she said, "have you talked to Sara or Allie since . . ."

I shook my head. This was something I did *not* want to get into with her.

"Max, maybe you should call—"

"I'll see them both at Sara's party. It's fine."

"I just think it'd be nice if—"

"Mom," I said.

"Okay," she said. "It's up to you."

What she was talking about happened a few weeks earlier. It started while Evan and I were waiting for the bus after school. Sara came over to tell us that she was putting us on her party's planning committee.

"What are you talking about?" Evan said. "It's just a party. Besides, we already gave you Extreme Musical Chairs," which is what we decided to call it.

"Get ice cream and order some pizzas," I said. "There. I just served on the planning committee."

"Chocolate ice cream and pepperoni pizza," Evan said. "Now *I've* served on the planning committee."

"I mean it," Sara said. She talks very evenly and pronounces every sound in every word, so she speaks more slowly than most people. But you pay attention. She also looks you in the eye, which can make you a little afraid of her sometimes.[7] "How about if you guys come over Saturday afternoon?" When you say something Sara doesn't agree with, she just pretends you didn't say it.

"Can't," I said. "I have to work."

---

[7] Well, it makes me a little afraid of her sometimes. She doesn't scare Evan.

"Right," she said. "Like you have a job."

"I do. I work in the store."

Her eyes got big. "I love you guys' store! You have such *cute stuff*!"

Oh no. I'd always known that sooner or later, girls my age would start coming into the store. Until now, it had been later. Now it was sooner. I mean, now it was now.

The bus was pulling up. "Yeah, whatever. Anyway, I have to work."

"Well, you go on breaks, don't you? You get to eat lunch? We can all meet at the food court at noon."

"'All'?" Evan said. "Who's 'all'?"

"You and Max and Allie and me."

"Oh, come on," Evan said. "I can't believe that you and Allie can't plan something by yourselves."

"This is more fun. And Allie's really nervous about the party, and I thought that maybe—"

The bus driver said, "If you're gonna get on, get on."

"Food court at noon!" Sara shouted as the doors whooshed shut behind us.

Saturday morning at 11:55, my mom said, "What do you mean, you forgot to bring your lunch?"[72] This was how I was going to get to go to the food court.

"I mean, I forgot to bring my lunch."

---

72 A lot of questions aren't really questions, because the person asking them doesn't want an answer. This type of question is actually a way of saying something. Like, "What do you think you're doing?" isn't really a question about what you think. My mom was saying she was mad because I forgot my lunch.

"Well, you've been warned about this," she said. "If you're going to eat that junk, you're going to have to spend your own money."

"Sorry."

"Don't tell me, tell your wallet. Your stomach might need a kind word too."

"It'll survive." I started out the back door.

"Half an hour," she said.

I said, "Forty-five minutes."

"Forty."

"Forty-five."

"Forty."

"Forty-three."

"All right," she said. "Be back in forty-three minutes."

"Round up to forty-five," I said. "That's what we do in math class. See you."

I took the secret passageway and came out on the other side of the food court. Sara, Allie, and Evan were already at a table. The instant I saw them, I got afraid I wouldn't have anything to say, or that I'd say something stupid. The feeling came out of nowhere. And these are people that I know pretty well.

"I thought you'd be coming from your parents' store," Sara said when she saw me walking up.

"I did," I said. There were only three chairs, so I pulled one over from the next table, sat down, and just started talking. I'd decided to try to be funny. "But I used a transporter. It breaks down your body into subatomic particles, then reassembles you where you want to be. But it's hard to get it just right. I tried to set the coordinates for the food court, but"—I pointed behind me—"I overshot, and . . . what?"

"Max," Sara said, "has anyone ever told you that you're insane?"

Before I could answer whatever it was I would have answered, Evan said, "Got any coins in your pocket?"

I said, "Sure."

"Let me see 'em."

I dug a quarter and a few pennies out my jeans and handed them over. He jingled them in his hand. "How come they're not hot? When you're in a transporter, any metal you're carrying heats up. So why—"

"Will you guys stop?" Sara had heard enough.

But Allie hadn't. She leaned forward and looked at me over those almost-invisible glasses. "What if you materialized inside a wall or something? Hmmm? Or halfway into the ground? Wouldn't that kill you?"

Now it was fun all of a sudden, and I relaxed just as fast as I'd gotten nervous a minute earlier. It felt just like it did when Allie and I were pretend-arguing about the scientific catalog. I sighed, like I had to explain something really obvious. "You have to make sure the transporter's safety lock is on. That's why you're supposed to be at least eighteen to operate one. So don't tell anybody."

Sara laughed. "I don't think you have to worry about that," she said.

"You must've been using some new-model transporter," Evan said as he handed the coins back to me, "because these are hardly even warm."

"It's an iPorter," I said. "They're a lot better than—"

"Okay, okay," Sara said. "Can we do a little planning now?"

"No," Evan said, "because we're going to do a little lunch-eating now."

Evan and I saved the table while Sara and Allie went to get their stuff. When they got back, we both headed for the Mexican place. I always pick Mexican.[73] One of the best things about it is that it goes so well with soda.[74]

Sara and Allie had both gotten Chinese something. I looked over at Sara as Evan and I were unwrapping our stuff. "Wow," I said. "You're really good with chopsticks."

She put them down and gave me that you're-an-alien stare again.

"Max," Allie said, "what's Sara's last name?"

"Chen," I said.

"And what kind of name is 'Chen'?" Allie asked, like I was a little boy.

"Chinese," I said. Then I said, "Oh."

"Now you're talking about my cousin," Sara said. We all looked at her.

"Rachel Oh," she said. "That's my cousin's name. Rachel Oh."

---

73 "You're going to get sick of it if you eat it all the time," my mom said. That's a good point. I'll probably be getting sick of it by the time I'm ninety-nine or a hundred.

74 According to my dad, free refills is one of the greatest advances in the history of civilization. "Max, my son," he said, "there was a time when people had to <u>pay</u> for a second cup of soda. Thank goodness you didn't have to live through that."

I was embarrassed about sounding so stupid, so I kind of went overboard trying to make up for it. "Really?" I said. "What a cool name. Rachel Oh."

"No, not *really*." Sara laughed. She picked up her chopsticks. "God, you'll believe anything."

It seemed like no matter which way the conversation went, I was going to sound like an idiot. I remembered what my mom said about certain times when the best thing you can do is concentrate on keeping your mouth closed, so while Sara, Allie, and Evan ate and talked, I opened my mouth only to take in two guacamole tacos, refried beans, and a 16-ounce suicide.

After a few minutes I got up to go for a suicide refill. Today it was Coke, Sprite, root beer, and lemonade. Four high school guys had just walked up to the next table, the one that now had three chairs.

"Hey," one of the guys said to me. He was really, really tall, with a backward baseball cap so far back on his head that the bill was actually over his neck. "Did you steal a chair from this table?"

I looked up at him. "No."[75]

"Well," he said, "are you still using it?"

"Yeah."

"It looked to me like you were leaving."

"I'm coming back," I said.

---

75 There's a saying: "Honesty is the best policy." But sometimes you have to tell a lie, or even a couple of lies, just to make it through the day alive. Anybody who says that's not true is lying.

He said, "What are you going to do about it when you come back and the chair's gone?"

"Don't come back at all," one of his buddies said. "That'll solve the problem."

I could feel myself starting to shake. I hated that this was happening in front of Sara and Allie.

I shoved the chair toward Evan. "Here," I said. "Save this for me, would you?" At least my voice wasn't shaking.

"Sure." Evan raised his feet and pushed them through the armrests, then plopped his legs down on the seat. Sara hung her orange bag over the back. I turned around and walked away fast. The Mexican place was in the other direction, just past the high school guys, but I thought I'd better take the long way around.

I took the same way back. Evan still had his legs across the chair, even though the high school guys had found a fourth one somewhere. Evan pulled his feet out, and I started to put my drink down. That's when the tall guy turned around, lifted one of his long legs, and kicked me in the butt. I crashed into the table. The cup flew out of my hand, and 16 ounces of suicide drenched the front of Allie's shirt.

Allie shrieked and tried to jump back out of her chair. It scooted a few inches, and then the back legs stuck on the floor, and she would have fallen over backward if Evan hadn't grabbed her arm. Sara was screaming at the high school guys, who were laughing and giving the tall guy high fives. People around us looked away: *just kids messing around.*

I looked at the guacamole smeared all over my right arm, then at Allie, who had her arms crossed over her chest, and had started to cry. Evan said he'd go for napkins, and took off.

"Allie, I'm sorry," I said. "Those guys—" I turned around. They were still laughing.

The tall guy suddenly acted all serious and concerned. "Is there a problem here, young man?" He spread his arms. "Is there anything we can do to help?" They all started up howling again.

Sara was bending down and talking to Allie. I didn't know what to do, except wait for Evan to get back with the napkins.

Sara stood up straight. "Max," she hissed, "come here a minute." I walked around the table. She cupped both hands around my ear and whispered, "You can see right through Allie's shirt, and she's not wearing anything underneath. We have to do something."

What I wanted to do was look at the front of Allie's shirt. I knew that was the wrong thing to be thinking, but it jumped into my mind and stuck there, and it took up all the space. There was no room left for any other thoughts at all. So I just stood there, trying to find an excuse to turn around and look in Allie's direction. At the same time, I was telling myself that I was a real creep.

Sara stepped back. "Come *on*," she said. "Let's get her out of here. Maybe we can find a jacket or something . . . Max?"

One of the high school guys yelled at Allie, "Hey— lookin' *good*!" Allie swiveled around in her chair so that her back was to them. She was still bent over, and now she was crying harder.

Finally my brain started working again, and the idea came to me.

When Evan got back with the napkins, I grabbed some and wiped the guacamole off my arm, but Sara told him to forget about cleaning the table. "We're going to form a human shield," she said. "Allie will be between you two, and I'll walk in front."

Evan said, "What—"

"Just go with it," Sara said. "Now, Allie, you stand up—" Allie shook her head. "This will work. For real. Just get up slowly—"

"No!"

"Listen, you can keep your arms in front of you. Just get up and turn around and stand right behind me, real close."

Allie lifted her head and looked at Sara, who nodded. Allie got up, arms clenched tight, her head down, and followed Sara to where we were standing.

"I wish I hadn't turned the transporter off," I said, "because—"

"No jokes," Sara said. "Just take us to one of those secret doors of yours."

The closest one was the one I'd come out of, next to the Mexican place. The human shield worked perfectly. As soon as I got us through the door, Sara said, "You guys go on ahead. We'll follow you." I always thought the corridors were spooky, but it was extra strange with the four of us walking along not saying a word. I could hear that Allie was still crying a little. A door opened, and a guy in a brown UPS uniform came out, wheeling a handcart with a couple of large boxes. I looked back and saw that Allie had turned to face a wall. We just stood around till he went by.

When we reached the back of the store, I unlocked the door and said, "You guys wait here."

My mom was up front, moving some shorts from one shelf to another. "Wow, that was nowhere near forty-five minutes," she said. "That's *fast* fast food."

"Mom," I said, "there's a little problem."

"Okay," she said after she opened the back door and saw Allie's shirt, "here's what we're going to do. Evan?"

"Yeah?"

"Thanks for your help. Now go home."

"Okay." He looked up and down the corridor. "How do I get out?"

"Just go through the front of the store," I said, and pointed. "This way."

He took a deep breath. He was going to have to walk all the way through a women's clothing store.

"Go on, kiddo," my mom said. "You'll live."[76]

She smiled at Sara and Allie. "Come on in," she said. Allie wasn't crying anymore, but you could sure tell she had been. My mom put her arm around her. "You're Allie, right? Allison?" Allie nodded. "Well, you're in luck. Some incredibly cool T-shirts came in today, and I bet we have a small one we can spare. Max?"

"Huh? What?"

---

[76] I called him later, and she was right.

"Go get a towel, please. Then get lost." A little while later she drove Sara and Allie home.

When I got into bed that night, I turned out the light, lay down—and felt something under my pillow.

The scientific catalog. Allie had kept it so long that I'd almost forgotten about it.

I turned the light back on, sat up, and for a few minutes I flipped through the pages without really looking at anything. I decided to keep it for a while. It felt good just holding it.

But one thing required an explanation.

"Mom!"

She opened the door and stuck her head in. "You still up? What?"

I held up the catalog. "Oh, that," she said. "Allie asked me to find a good place for it. How'd I do?"

I tossed the catalog—*thunk!*—on the floor. "Pretty good, I guess."

She leaned against the doorway and folded her arms. "You did some good yourself today. You and Evan both, and Sara, helping out a friend like that."

I shrugged.

"No, I mean it, Max. You can't imagine how embarrassing and awful that was for her. Now that I think of it, they're all really good kids. And so are you."

"I've got you all fooled," I said. "I put on a good act."

"Well, that's the secret," she said. "Keep it up." She turned out the light and closed the door. A week later school was out, and two weeks after that we packed up and headed for the camp.

Part Two
Camping

chapter

COSTUME CHANGE;
BIG FIVE;
NATURAL
TROUBLEMAKERS

*G*ood kid. My mom was right. That's me.

That *was* me, anyway.

We got to the camp early in the afternoon. It was in the mountains, all right. The last half hour of the drive was on a twisty, winding road, with guardrails to keep cars from going over million-foot cliffs.[77] [78] Gi-mongous pine trees everywhere.

When we drove in, counselors met us with a cold pitcher of what they called "bug juice," but it tasted

---

77 "Fifty-foot cliffs" isn't funny.

78 When I was little, I was sure we were *going* to miss a turn and go right through a guardrail and over the edge. "Don't look if it scares you, sweetie," my mom would say. But you <u>have</u> to look, right?

just like lemonade to me. They showed us this huge bell sitting on a tree stump in front of the dining hall, which they rang as a wake-up call and to announce breakfast, lunch, and dinner, but if we heard it any other time, or if it just kept ringing, that meant there was some kind of emergency. Don't bother with your cell, because there's no coverage.

As we were signing in, I peeked at a clipboard that had a list of campers and their ages, to see how many people my age were there. A tall, redheaded counselor with the nametag "Jake" saw me and laughed.

"It's not a state secret," he said, and spun the clipboard around on the table so I could read it. I flipped through the pages and saw that there were kids as old as sixteen and as young as three, and a whole lot of seven, eight, nine, and ten. But what I was looking for was twelve or thirteen, and there were . . . let's see . . . there's two twelves, and there's a thirteen, and—

"Okay, we got our cabin," my mom said. "Let's go."

It had wood floors, wood walls, and a canvas roof that made it look like a giant tent. The first thing we did after moving all our stuff in was to string our old hammock between two fat trees. I climbed in just as my dad finished tying the last knot.

"Not yet," he said. He put out a hand to stop my swinging back and forth. "We still have to unpack everything. Out."

I got out. He got in.

"Hey!" I said.

"Long trip," he said. "Driver needs to recover."

"What about unpacking?"

"Good idea. Don't let me stop you."

I grabbed the edge of the hammock and started to tip him over and out.

"I've got one word for you, Max," he said. "'Commissary.' Think about it."

The commissary was the little store where they sold ice cream and sno-cones and sodas and energy bars and flashlights and hats and camp T-shirts and sweatshirts—all kinds of stuff. Your parents put in a deposit, and then you could go and pick out whatever you wanted, and the guy would just subtract the price from the deposit. We'd been talking about how much they were going to put in for me.

"You were up to twenty-five dollars," my dad said. "A hammock tip-over would knock that down to twenty. So if you think it's worth five dollars, go ahead."

But I was already walking away. There was nobody anywhere near my age in the cabins right around us, but three guys and two girls were carrying towels and walking along the dirt path toward the swimming pool.

Now or never, I said to myself. I decided to go with *now.*

I went into the cabin and dug around till I found the old T-shirts we had brought to use as rags. I picked one that was reddish orange and had a bunch of small holes. That made it easy to tear a wide strip out of it.

"What in the world are you doing?" my mom said. She was putting our sleeping bags on the cots.

I wrapped the strip around my head and tied a knot in back.

"Ah," she said. "Headband."

Then I rolled up the sleeves of my T-shirt as far I could.

"You'll need sunscreen on those shoulders."

I hardly ever wore sunglasses, but my dad always brought extras. I grabbed a pair and put them on.

"Young man," my mom said, "have you seen Max?"

I pulled the swim trunks from my duffel bag. "Never heard of him," I said. "And turn around." I changed, grabbed a towel, and took off for the pool.

When I went through the shower room, I heard a rustling sound, almost like a whisper, and looked up. There was no roof, and pine branches were swaying way up overhead. This shower room wasn't even a little bit gross and disgusting, like most of them are. The camp was looking better all the time.

I walked out onto the pool deck still wearing the sleeveless-looking T-shirt, the headband, and the sunglasses. The group I'd seen a few minutes earlier had spread towels at the far end, on some grass behind the diving board. The old Max would have hung around and waited for them to notice him, and maybe tried to work his way into a game in the pool or something. Max 2.0 didn't operate like that.

Right away I got lucky. I was walking along the edge of the pool, straight toward them, wondering what I was going to say, when a little kid who was hanging on to a ladder in the deep end looked up at me and squinted. He put his hand up to block the sun and said, "Hey, why are you wearing a headband?"

"Where I come from, everybody wears a headband," I said in a loud, non–Max 1.0 voice.

"Where's that?"

I hadn't stopped walking, so I called back over my shoulder, "Timbuktu."

"Huh?" he said. But by that time I was past the diving board and was standing in front of those five kids. They had stopped talking and were checking me out. I tossed my towel down and kicked it open.

"So I guess none of you guys are from Timbuktu," I said, and sat down. I could hardly believe that I'd actually done it. But there I was.

Silence for three, four, five seconds. Then one of the girls, who had long, curly brown hair and a bright orange swimsuit, said, "I'm Maddy."

"Josh," said the guy sitting next to her, with curly brown hair almost as long. He looked a lot like her. Brother and sister? Maybe even twins?

Maddy pointed to the other girl, who was dripping wet. She must have jumped in the pool and gotten right out again. She had a black bikini, but no telling what she looked like, because she'd put a towel over her head and was furiously drying her hair. "And she's, um . . . oh, jeez, I'm sorry . . ."

"Kim," the girl said from behind the towel. She pulled it off. Very short black hair. Very, *very* pale blue eyes. "And as Bart Simpson says, who the hell are you?"

I forced myself to look right into those two pale

blue circles of light, but it wasn't easy. Maddy was pretty pretty,[79] but Kim was so beautiful that I just froze. I said to myself, "Come *on*." So I laced my fingers together, turned my hands inside out, and managed to crack five knuckles, a new record. "Max," I said.

"Mad Max!" one of the other guys hooted. That's the title of a superviolent movie, where the hero, Max, goes kind of crazy in this world of the future.[80]

"You got that right," I said. "And as Kim says, who the hell are you?"

Everybody hooted at that. I amazed myself at what I'd said—mentioning Kim so casually, like I already knew her, and throwing back that "Who the hell are you?" stuff. The words just came out. I was already feeling comfortable in the Max 2.0 costume.

The other two were Bryce, a little guy[81] with rectangular gray-framed glasses that didn't sit quite straight, and Connor, who looked about twice his size. "Call him Connie," Bryce said, and Connor slapped him on the side of the head. In the next couple of minutes I learned that Bryce and Connor's families had been coming to this camp for years, so they'd known each

---

79 Can you say that? It makes sense, right? So I guess you can.

80 It's rated R, so I'm not allowed to see it. That doesn't mean I haven't seen it.

81 Anybody smaller than me is a little guy.
Anybody bigger than me is a big guy.

other practically forever. The other three were all new. Maddy and Josh were cousins, not twins.

Connor was looking at them, first one, then the other. "But you're about the same age, right?"

"Exactly the same age," Maddy said.

"Born on the same day," Josh said. They sounded like they'd said it about two hundred times.[82]

"So you guys are what?" Kim said. "Eight years old? Seven?"

"Six," Maddy said.

Josh balled up a T-shirt and threw it at her. She swatted it away and laughed. "We're thirteen," Josh said. "Double birthday just last week."

"Hey, Mad Max," Bryce said. "What are you? Nineteen?"

"Twenty-two," I said. "Too bad you guys aren't old enough to drink any of the beer I brought."

Bryce said, "Beer?"

Connor said, "You've got beer? Really?"

"Yeah, guys," Kim said. "He's got beer just like he's twenty-two." She turned to look at me. "Let me guess," she said. "You're . . . fourteen."

Unbelievable! Fantastic! Unbelievably fantastic! She thinks I'm fourteen! Something I was doing was working. I decided to make it more realistic by being *almost* fourteen.

---

82 When I told Maddy that later, she said it was more like ten thousand times. Obviously, she was exaggerating. See? Everybody does it.

"Not till November," I said. But I'd still added a year.

"So you're going to be a freshman like me, right?" Kim said. No, but I wasn't going to say anything. "All these other guys are eighth graders."

"I don't know about Connor," Bryce said. "Hey, Connor, did you pass seventh grade?"

But Connor was staring at Maddy and Josh again. "Wait a second. You guys are cousins and you were born on the same day?" He pointed at them and looked around at all of us. "How weird is *that*?"

I remembered how everybody always said the same things about how I'm a tween, and how tired I get hearing it.

"Not that weird," I said. "It's just a coincidence. Everybody's gotta be born sometime, right?" I stood up and pulled off my sunglasses and T-shirt. "What, do you guys just sit here? That's what it's going to be like all week?" And I walked over to the pool and didn't stop. Just stepped right off the edge into the deep end, and disappeared.

Before I got back up to the surface, there were explosions all around me. Five of them. I came up first, and shook my head to get the wet hair out of my—nope: no hair in my eyes. Mad Max wears a headband. Even in the pool.

Mad Max, I said to myself. *Whoa!*

chapter

IN TROUBLE ALREADY; *UN*–MAD MAX; FOOD FIGHT

We wore ourselves out in the pool, with inner-tube fights (you have to tip the other guy over) and keep-away with a mostly deflated volleyball. Later one of the lifeguards[83] came over to where we were lying on our towels. She said that her name was Camille, that she was the head lifeguard, and next time we go in the pool would we please take it down a notch or two, because adults are trying to relax and do laps, and to please watch out because there are small children in the pool, too.

"We can't help it," I said, and it was like I was

---

83 Lifeguards seem like they're all best friends, and you get the feeling they do nothing but hang out with each other, and party all night, and have more fun in one summer than you'll have in the whole rest of your life. It's hard not to feel like a dweeb when you're around a lifeguard.

hearing somebody named Mad Max talking. "We're just natural troublemakers."

"Yeah," Kim said. "It's out of our control."

"Oh, that's wonderful," Camille said with a sigh. "That's just what I wanted to hear."

"Sorry," Josh said.

Maddy said, "We won't be a problem." She looked at Kim and then at me. "Right?" She laughed. "Will we be a problem?"

"Nope."

"Nope."

"Nope," Connor added.

"Yep," said Bryce. "I mean, nope."

"Great," Camille said. "We want you to have a good time, but without killing anybody, if possible."

"That's not so easy," I said.

Camille turned to walk away. "Try," she said.

We all got toasted, lying there in the sun. We jumped into the pool one last time, then headed for the commissary to get something to drink. Nobody bothered to dry off—we just dripped our way along the path.

"Did your parents put any money on deposit for you?" Bryce asked as we were walking up to the store.

"Uh-oh," said Maddy. She looked at Josh. "Mine didn't. Did yours?"

"I don't think they have yet," he said.

I said, "Mine either."

"No problem," Bryce said. "I'll buy this time—one of you guys buys next." We'd only been together for a couple of hours, but we were already a posse. And one of the members was Mad Max.

We split up to go back to our cabins and let our parents know we weren't dead or anything.

"You're not going to eat with us?" my mom said. She was putting up a clothesline between two trees not being used by the hammock. "This is a family camp, remember?"

"I eat with you guys almost every night," I said. "Come *on*."

"What's with the headband?" my dad said as he walked out of the cabin. He was kind of staggering, which meant he'd just gotten up from a nap.

"Headband Max says he's not eating with us."

My dad rubbed his face. He was still trying to wake up. "Great," he said. "We can have a romantic dinner, just the two of us and whatever six or eight other people end up sitting at our table."

"Come on, Mom," I said.

"Are those my sunglasses?" my dad said.

"Mom?"

"You know your shoulders got a little sunburned," she said.

"Mom?"

"Oh, go ahead, sit with your new friends," she said. "But that spoils all our plans for you not to have any fun while you're here."

"I know," I said. "Nice try." I took off the damp headband and hung it on the clothesline, then eased myself into the hammock. My dad was still kind of just wandering around. I twisted my head around and looked at him. "Gimme a push?" He got me swinging. I put the sunglasses up on my head and closed my eyes.

It had been so easy for me to become Mad Max. But as soon as I got back to our cabin, I'd started arguing with my mother about where I was going to sit in the stupid dining hall. I felt like the old Max,[84] almost like I was a little kid again, and I didn't like it. Mad Max wasn't exactly the person I wanted to be for the rest of my life, but so far he had made five new friends in half an afternoon. I was going to keep him around for a while.

Especially because of the way he'd—I mean, I'd—acted so cool around Kim. Before, like when I felt uncomfortable up close to Sara, and then Allie, I just sort of shut up, or if I talked, I usually said something dumb, and that made me even more uncomfortable. Today I was able to push my way through it. And it worked. Nothing bad happened when I forced myself to be more out there. In fact, something good happened: I impressed a beautiful girl, and got a great new name to go along with my new personality.

At six o'clock the big bell rang for dinner, but I showed up a few minutes after everyone in camp had poured into the dining hall, because I was Mad Max and I knew my friends would save me a place. I was also late because I didn't remember my headband until

---

84 Alice wouldn't care which Max I was.

I was halfway there, and had to run back to the cabin to get it, then run all the way to the dining hall. Then I had to wait till I could catch my breath, because Mad Max was too cool to show up all red-faced and panting.

"Feeding time at the mountain zoo," I heard one of the counselors say as I walked in. There were three long rows of picnic tables, every one of them crammed with people. The air was so thick with the roar of everybody talking at the tops of their voices, and little kids screaming, and the steam from all the food, and the smell of all the food,[85] that walking through the dining hall felt almost like swimming. I spotted my mom and dad right away, at a table with some other parents. I guess their kids had deserted them, too.

"Max! Over here!" Arms waved from a table all the way in the back. I weaved around the servers wheeling cartloads of food, which was harder than it sounds because I'd decided to stick with the sunglasses look, so it was extra dark in there.

"Feeding time at the mountain zoo," I said as I climbed in next to Kim. I looked at the table and acted surprised. "Wow! We get plates and silverware! I thought they'd just throw huge chunks of meat at us, and we'd all have to fight for it."

Kim elbowed me hard. It felt good. "Hey!" I said. "That's my sore arm. Now I'll never recover." Actually,

---

85 They didn't serve spaghetti even once all week, if that's what you're thinking.

it had been more than a month since Sara had slugged me, and the bruise was long gone. But that just sort of popped out of my mouth. It wasn't true, but so what? Mad Max says whatever he wants.

Maddy said, "How'd you hurt your arm?"

"Some loser girl hit me," I said. Everybody but Maddy laughed.

"Really?" she said. "What did you do to deserve it?"

"Hey, hey!" Josh said, making a T with his hands to signal Time-out. "We're all friends here. No fighting till the end of the week."

"Yeah," said Kim. "Then, on the last day we can get into huge arguments, and swear we'll never speak to each other again, and all go home really mad."

"Good idea!" Bryce said. "Connor, write that down somewhere."

"How about if I write it on your forehead?" He got Bryce in a headlock, and they started wrestling and halfway knocked over a pitcher of bug juice, which Josh grabbed before it tipped over completely. Maddy, Josh, and I started soaking up spilled juice with paper napkins, but Connor and Bryce kept wrestling until finally they slammed into a couple of parents sitting at the table behind them, who turned around and told them to knock it off.

Josh called out, "Sorry!"

Kim looked at him and sort of half laughed. "Are you, like, the hall monitor or something?"

"No, I am," I said. I pulled a couple more wads of napkins out of the holder and tossed them at Bryce and Connor. "You two morons help clean up, or I'll be the one you have to fight." I put my elbows on the table and leaned forward. "And Mad Max fights *dirty*."

They laughed. "Great," Connor said, starting to mop up some juice. "So do we."

"Dirty fighting!" Kim said. "Gotta love it."

The servers reached our table and started handing out trays of food. Josh took one and stabbed three pieces of chicken, one after the other, dumped them on his plate, and passed the tray. "You guys can fight or plan fights," he said. "I'm eating."

Maddy took the tray from him, passed it along, and didn't say anything at all.

chapter

"CRAZY IS GOOD"; TAKE A HIKE; SHOW TIME

The camp had a lot of activities,[86] just like my mom said, but we all hung out at the pool, and at the tables next to the commissary, and by the cabin of whoever's parents weren't around. Connor and Bryce bragged about all the wild things they did and all the trouble they got into at school. I guess they did do wild things and get into trouble at school, but I was pretty sure they were making up half the stuff to

---

86 One time when I told my dad that I'd never seen anybody actually playing shuffleboard, anywhere, he grabbed my arm and whispered that shuffleboard courts are actually mini-landing strips for tiny UFOs. "But don't ever, ever let anyone hear you say that," he said, still whispering. "This is a very serious matter." Then he let go of my arm and said in a normal voice, "We will never speak of this again." When we walked by the shuffleboard court the first day at camp, he looked at me out of the corner of his eye, put a finger to his lips, and went "Shhhhh."

impress Kim and Maddy. Maddy and Josh and I liked Harry Potter and Lemony Snicket, the books even more than the movies, so we talked about the characters and our favorite lines. But after a while Kim always said, "What is this? English class?"

So we'd switch to music and movies. Kim and Maddy were in a constant semi-argument about Rupert Grint, who Kim was in love with, and Matt Smith from *Dr. Who*, who Maddy said was the best actor who ever lived, and that cute doesn't matter, but Matt Smith's cuter anyway. Every day, sooner or later, it'd be a Rupert Grint vs. Matt Smith smackdown. The only way we could get them to stop was to talk about football in really loud voices.

We also spent a lot of time commenting on every adult who came anywhere near us. That was fun, and it got even more fun when Josh invented the Future Game.

"That's you in twenty years," he said to Connor as a huge man walked by the commissary carrying floatie noodles, a bunch of towels, and a canvas tote bag, as two little kids ran around him begging for ice cream. "See? You're even wearing the same color swim trunks."

At the pool that afternoon, Connor pointed to a tall, pale, skinny man who was always sitting in the shade reading a book while his wife ran after their little girl, smearing sunscreen on her and yelling at her not to go in the deep end. He never once looked up. Connor said, "Tell me that's not Josh in twenty years."

"That's Josh," Bryce said.

"That's Josh if he ever finds anybody lame enough to marry him," Kim said. Josh ignored her, but he didn't look too happy.

We checked out every adult to see who the rest of us would end up being most like. I wanted them to find some out-there, unusual, interesting person and say that was me in twenty years, but the only adults around were parents, so there wasn't anybody like that. Instead they all agreed I'd be most like my father, because it turned out that he'd seen Connor and Bryce near the shuffleboard court and told them the same thing he'd told me, about it being an alien landing strip.[87]

Maddy said, "He's as crazy as you are."

"Oh, great," I said. "I'm my father."

"Hey," Maddy said. I looked over, and she was smiling at me. "Crazy is good."

I started to smile back, then looked away, embarrassed. *Crazy is good.* I liked that. Thanks, Maddy.

The third day, our parents got together and signed all of us up for a half-day hike to a small lake.

"I told my mom I'm not going. Period. End of conversation," Kim said. She was at camp with just her mother. Nobody asked her where her father was, and she never mentioned him. We were sitting on some huge rocks that were more like boulders right behind Josh's

---

[87] "I thought that was a big secret," I said to my dad later. "It was," he said, "but I've decided that we have to let people know. Humanity's existence is at stake." I said, "So you think Connor and Bryce can help save humanity?" "Hmmm," he said. "Probably not. Good point."

family's cabin, which was next to Maddy's. Maddy was inside her cabin playing cards with her two little sisters while their parents were at the pool for some bizarro adult exercise class.

"They're leaving for that stupid hike at six in the morning," Connor said. "As if."

Bryce said, "My dad told me I was going whether I wanted to or not. That's jacked up. I'm staying in my sleeping bag. What's he going to do, carry me?"

"I'm going," Maddy called from next door. I hadn't realized she could hear us, but then, the cabins are half canvas.

"Have fun by yourself!" Kim yelled. She looked at Josh. "No, wait, I bet you're going. Cousins stick together, right?" Kim hated Josh. You could tell.

Josh shrugged. "The hiking counselor says the lake up there is—"

Kim pretended to be yawning. "Sounds *fascinating*. Be sure to take lots of pictures." Connor and Bryce laughed. Then she said, "What about you?"

I kind of wanted to go, but I was thinking that it wasn't something Mad Max would do. "I haven't made up my mind yet," I said. "But I have till ten minutes to six tomorrow morning to figure it out."

"I bet your parents make you go," Bryce said.

I leaned back on the boulder and tilted my face toward the sun and closed my eyes. What I saw was an image of myself, of how I looked to them right now: headband, sunglasses, rolled-up sleeves—a really interesting, crazy guy they called Mad Max. I felt the sun's heat on my face. I said slowly, "Nobody makes me go anywhere."

"You didn't go on the hike?" my mom whispered the next morning when she woke up and saw me still lying on my cot. "I heard your alarm go off."

"Nah," I whispered back. "Didn't feel like it."

"Well, I can certainly understand that. Why hike when you can hang out?"

My dad half sat up in his sleeping bag. Their cots were right next to each other. "Why what? Huh? What?"

"Why nothing," my mom said. "Go back to sleep." She put her hand on the top of his head and pushed down, just like cops on TV do when they're putting somebody into the backseat of a police car. He sank down and started snoring. "No snoring," she said, and he stopped.

When I'd shut off the alarm, the clock had fallen over on its face. I picked it up. Almost seven. Breakfast wasn't till eight, so I lay back down and put my hands behind my head. It had been morning for a while, but now the sun was streaming through the trees overhead, lighting up the canvas tent-ceiling and making leafy shadows that moved a little in the breeze. This was only our fourth day at the camp, but it felt like we'd been there a lot longer. Little kids were running around outside, and I could recognize the voices of the parents who were yelling at them.[88]

---

88 "Be quiet and get in here right now! People are trying to sleep!" And not once all week did the kids be quiet and get in there right now.

I met up with Kim and Connor and Bryce at breakfast. Then we hung out at Kim's cabin. Then we went to the pool. Then we went to lunch. Then we went to the commissary. Then we went to the pool again. Then we hung out at Bryce's cabin.

We didn't see Maddy and Josh till dinner. "We got back and crashed," Josh said. "I just woke up a few minutes ago. It was a long drive just to get to the trail, and then it was a long hike up to the lake. And it was *hot*."

"But the lake was awesome," Maddy said. "The water was freezing, but we were so hot we jumped in anyway. It was, *ZAP!* Like an electric shock. Then it felt unbelievably good. But you can't stand it for very long. We climbed up on some rocks and sat in the sun."

"Then we ate lunch, jumped back in for a minute, and started back," Josh said. "And hey," he said to Kim, "Good thing you reminded me to take my camera. Check these out." He shoved his camera about two inches in front of her face and started clicking through the shots as fast as he could. He disliked her as much as she disliked him.

"I'm *so* sorry I missed it," Kim said. She wasn't even pretending to look at the pictures. "Sad face, sad face."

I *was* sorry I missed it. I was picturing Maddy in her orange swimsuit, sitting on a rock by a lake.

Camille, the lifeguard, came by the table to remind us that at eight thirty there was going to be a movie at the outdoor theater in a public campground a little ways away.

"What movie?" Bryce said. "*Hannah Montana*?"

"I think it's *Raiders of the Lost Ark*," Camille said. "I hope that's not too babyish for you."

"Hey, I'm Indiana Max," I said. "That Indiana Jones guy stole my name."

"Well, maybe there's an Indiana Max movie next week, but we're walking over to see this one at eight if you guys want to come. And thanks for the cupcakes," she said as she snatched a couple off the table and we all said, "Hey!" She walked away laughing.

"I bet the people who made the *Mad Max* movie stole that name from you, too, huh?" Bryce said.

"Yeah," I said. "When I turn twenty-one, I'm going to sue everybody. I'll be rich."

"OOOOOooooo!" Kim said. "Rich!" She was sitting next to me, and she grabbed my right arm with both her hands and pulled us together and put her head on my shoulder. "We're gonna get married, right?"

"Uhhhhhhh," I said. No girl had ever held on to me like that, and it kind of made my brain spin for a few[89] seconds. "Sure," I finally said. "You can be my third wife." Connor and Bryce howled and held up hands for me to high-five. Kim elbowed me again, but she was laughing. Mad Max!

By eight it had cooled off a lot, but we could still feel the heat of the day rising from the asphalt road. Kim was walking between Bryce and Connor. That

---

89 About four.

bothered me. I didn't want to look at them, so I hurried ahead to be with Josh and Maddy. They were talking to Camille. She asked them the usual question.

"Cousins," Maddy said.

"Born on the same day," Josh said.

But Camille also asked them things I hadn't thought about. Like, why they spent so much time together. "I'd think you'd be fighting," Camille said, "or at least getting on each other's nerves or something. But you seem like you're best friends."

"Sometimes it *is* almost like we're twins,"[90] Maddy said. "A lot of times I start to say something, he says it instead. And we're always texting each other at exactly the same time."

"But we don't actually see each other all that much," Josh said. "We live in different parts of town, and go to different schools."

"Oh, so that's it," Camille said. "You never get a *chance* to get sick of each other."

"Until this week," Maddy said. "I was thinking about killing him on the hike. There was this one perfect-size rock, and I thought, 'I can pick this up, and *bam!*'"

---

90 Some guys at school said that everybody has a double, like an identical twin, living somewhere on earth. I told my dad, who said, "Max, sit down and think about that for five minutes." About five minutes later I said, "It doesn't make any sense, does it?" He said, "Nope." I said, "So why do people believe it?" He said, "Because they don't sit down and think about it for five minutes."

"Well," Josh said to her, "I was going to drown *you* in the lake."

Camille laughed. "And you, Max," she said, "what's with the blue headband? I thought orange was your color."

"No holes in this one," I said. "I wanted to get dressed up for the movie."

The seats at the outdoor theater were rows of benches arranged in kind of a quarter circle. Off to the left, toward the lake, a fat wedge of silver moon was sitting on top of a pine tree. There must've been a hundred people there. The benches were almost full, and a lot of families had brought beach chairs. Josh and Maddy ended up a few rows in front of the rest of us, because there wasn't room for us to all sit together. I made sure I was next to Kim. I didn't even pretend to be casual about it—when we got there, I stuck right next to her. I tried to imagine myself doing this back home, with Allie, but I couldn't make it seem real.

A woman stood in front of the screen and welcomed everybody, and said that there'd be a cartoon before the movie, and that the little store just down the road was open till ten, and that it sold popcorn on movie nights, and—

Connor and Kim and I were out of our seats and running, while Bryce stayed to save our places. "Get me some!" he yelled after us. We beat the million[91]

---

91 More like twenty.

other people who had the same idea. We had just paid for the popcorn when I remembered Maddy and Josh.

"Let 'em get their own," Kim said.

"Yeah," Connor said, and slapped me on the head. "They snoozed, they loozed."

I was still standing at the counter. Kim tugged at the sleeve of my T-shirt. "Come *on*," she said, so I did.

chapter

DORK BRAIN;
PUT A SOCK ON IT;
MOON SHADOWS

When the movie was over I stood up and looked for Josh and Maddy, but Connor tapped me on the shoulder. "Me and Bryce got this idea, bro."

"Okay," I said, still looking around.

Bryce said, "Kim's in on it too. She goes, 'I'll walk back with those two goodie-goodies to get them out of the way.'"

"In on what?" I said, and they both went, *"Shhhhhh!"*

They pulled me over behind some pine trees while Kim, Josh, and Maddy looked for us—Kim was faking it—and finally headed back. In a few minutes everybody else was gone too. "Okay," I said, "tell me."

Bryce said, "We're gonna steal the bell."

"Tonight," Connor said.

We started walking back to the camp. Their plan was to use Bryce's dad's crowbar to pry the bell loose from the tree stump, then hide it somewhere. When the counselors went to ring it in the morning, there'd be nothing there. They'd have to go around to every cabin to wake people up for breakfast.

"This place is so freaking dull," Connor said. "It's time something happened."

Bryce said, "You in?"

Connor said, "Oh, yeah, Mad Max is in."

"Oh, yeah," I said. "Mad Max is in."

Most of the families would be asleep by ten, they said, because of the little kids. Counselors stay up later, but they have to get up early, so one o'clock should be safe.

"That bell looks pretty heavy," Bryce said. "It'll take three of us to carry it. Kim's gonna be the lookout."

"Carry it where?" I said.

"Don't know yet. Someplace where it'll take them a while to find it."

Connor said, "It'd be cool if we could, like, put it on top of the dining hall."

Bryce said, "How are we going to do that, dork brain? We're barely going to be able to lift it."

"Oh . . . yeah," Connor said. "Yeah, but it'd be cool anyway."[92]

"Dork brain," Bryce said.

"Shut up!" Connor said. "You come up with something better."

"Dork brain."

---

92 Connor was dumber than Bryce, but not by much.

Connor lunged at him, but Bryce twisted away and ran up the dark road. "Dork brain!"

"Shut up!"

"Both of you shut up," I said. While they'd been acting like idiots, I'd realized that I could be in charge here. This was going to be *my* operation. All I had to do was start giving orders. And I knew I could: I was Mad Max. I could *feel* it.

Also, I had a killer idea. As soon as I decided to take over, it just came to me. When we caught up with Bryce, I adjusted my headband and said, "The pool."

They both said, "What?"

I said, "We carry it to the pool, and dump it in the deep end."

Bryce said, "Omigod! That's it!"

Connor said, "Omigod! That's it!"[93]

The rest of the way back, I told them how it was going to work. Put some clothes and shoes outside your cabin. If your parents wake up while you're sneaking out, say you're going to the bathroom. One of us—Connor—has to bring some heavy socks to put over the bell's clapper,[94] so it won't clang when we're moving it. No flashlights because they just attract attention, and anyway, there's enough moon for us to see what we're doing.

---

93 Connor was probably too dumb to think of "Omigod! That's it!" on his own.

94 I didn't know the word "clapper" at the time, so what I said was "clanger-thingy."

ing out, like I was a criminal mastermind or something. Well, I knew I wasn't *that*. But I was different from who I'd been before. I'd *made* myself different. And I was more excited about that than I was about stealing the bell.

And I was plenty excited about stealing the bell.

We got back around eleven fifteen. My parents were reading, waiting up for me. While I changed for bed, they asked how the movie was and I said fine, and they asked if I had fun and I said yes.[95] When I went to brush my teeth, I carried my clothes and shoes with me. I was sure they wouldn't notice, and they didn't. I came back in, and my dad turned out the light. In a few minutes he was snoring. My mom must've been asleep too, because she didn't jiggle him or tell him to turn over and knock it off.

There was no danger of my falling asleep, because I was as awake as I've ever been while lying in bed. At ten minutes to one I slipped out of the sleeping bag and out the door. I went around to the back of the cabin to get my stuff and, brilliant me, walked right into the clothesline. Down I went, on my back in the dirt.

Somebody snorted, trying not to laugh out loud. "Good one, Maximillian." It was Kim, whispering.

_____

95 If scientists used a scanner to show your brain while you're answering most of the questions your parents ask, only about 1/800 of the picture would light up.

She'd been waiting for me! And here I was, acting like a clown, wearing just the boxer shorts I sleep in.

I got up and brushed off dirt and twigs and pine needles. I didn't know what to say, so I just found my clothes and started pulling them on. I could feel Kim watching. When I sat down to put on my shoes, she came over and sat next to me. She squeezed my knee. "Hey, Maximillian," she whispered, "are you okay? You fell pretty hard."

I nodded, and tried to act like this was just a regular thing for me, sitting next to a girl in the dark, in the middle of the night. And was it great or what, that she'd given me a private nickname? I finished tying my shoes and whispered, "Let's go."

Connor and Bryce were already there. The bell hung from a metal frame, and they were working at prying out the huge nails that held the frame to the stump. Connor was working at it, that is. Bryce was just standing there.

I said,[96] "Did you check to see if anybody's around?"

"Everybody's asleep, just chill," Connor said. He was leaning on the crowbar, bouncing a little. The nail

---

96 We all whispered, but if you read "He whispered" or "She whispered" more than a couple of times, it starts to sound so stupid that you can't pay attention to what's going on in the story. Watch: I whispered, "Did you check to see if anybody's around?" . . . "Everybody's asleep, just chill," Connor whispered. . . . "C'mon," I whispered to Bryce. See? So I just wrote "said" every time. Go with it.

squeeeeeaked and groaned and popped out. "One down, three to go," he said, and started on the next one.

"C'mon," I said to Bryce. "Let's check out the pool." Since Kim was the lookout, she'd stay with Connor.

The pool was on the other side of a circle of five or six cabins. We could carry the bell around them, no problem, but I hadn't thought about the pool's chain-link fence. We tried the doors to the shower rooms: locked.

Bryce tapped on the door to the men's section. "This is nothing," he said. He rammed into it with his shoulder, then rammed into it harder. There was a splintering sound, and the door flew open and banged against the wall.

"Think you could make any *more* noise?" I said as we ran around to the other side of the pool. We hid behind the equipment shack for a few long minutes, but nobody came. When we got back to the bell, Connor had all the nails out. I said, "You brought socks to cover the clanger-thingy, right?"

"Dammit!" he said. "No, I didn't."

I looked at his feet and said, "Yes, you did."

While Connor was sitting on the ground taking his shoes off, I reached under the bell and grabbed the clapper. Connor handed Kim a sock. "Ever hear of doing laundry?" she said.

I put first that sock, then the other one[97] over the clapper. Connor finished putting his sockless shoes

---

97 Just as smelly. No big surprise there.

back on, stood up, and brushed off his butt. "All clear," Kim said. The plan was for Bryce and me to carry one side of the frame, Connor the other. Connor walked over to his side, and we all got ready.

"Lift!" he said.

It was heavy, all right. We staggered down the dirt road that went around the cabins. Every now and then the bell would swing in the frame a little and the clapper would go *clunk!* So the sock idea worked.

"Hey," I said, "I thought we . . . were going to put this . . . on top of the dining hall."

"Don't . . . make . . . me . . . laugh!" Bryce kind of squeaked. His glasses had come off one ear and were barely hanging by the other one. A few steps later he said, "Gotta put it down, gotta put it DOWN!" We shuffled to the side of the road and started lowering it, but Bryce's glasses finally fell off and he let go, so Connor and I had to too.

"Fail!" Connor said, giving Bryce a shove. "Who's the dork brain now?"

Bryce was panting. "I can't get a good grip on it," he said, putting his glasses back on, "and my hands—"

"You and I can take turns," Kim said. "Come on."

We made it about halfway around the cabins before we all had to rest. We set the bell by the side of the road again. "This is just so unbelievably great," Bryce said. "When the counselors see—"

Kim held up a hand. *"Shhhhh!* Somebody's . . ." She pointed down the road.

He was still a ways off, but he was definitely heading in our direction. "Get the bell!" Connor said, but there wasn't time. We crept over to the moon shadows of the nearest pine tree, then had to freeze because whoever it was came around a short bend in the road.

It was Jake, the tall, redheaded counselor I'd talked to the first day. If there was enough light for me to recognize him, he had to be able to see us. And even if he didn't notice us in the shadows, there was the bell, just sitting there. I could actually see the bent shape of the moon reflected in its curved metal. I got ready to yell to everybody to just run. Maybe he wouldn't be able to tell who we were.

The sound of his feet crunching on the road . . . then it seemed like he was looking at the bell, but not slowing down . . . then he was looking past the bell—*he didn't even see it!* Then he was walking away. Then he was gone. We all collapsed in the pine needles.

"God, I just knew we were dead," Bryce said.

"Nope," I said, "still alive."

"And the bell still needs to go to the pool," Kim said. "Come on."

A few minutes later it sat by the diving board, just a few feet from the spot where I'd met them—was it just three days ago?

We agreed on a one-two-three-HEAVE! Kim joined Connor on his side, so she could be part of the throwing-in ceremony. "All together now," I said as we picked the bell up for the last time. We swung it back and forth, the clapper *clunk!*-ing, and counted "One . . . two . . . three . . . HEAVE!"

It went about two feet at most, *ker-SPLASHED!* into the water sideways, and went straight down fast. It landed on its side and rolled down one way, then another, dragging the frame with it, till it came to a stop next to the drain.

"Awesome!" Connor said. "We're gonna be famous."

"Nobody talks," Kim said. "Seriously. Nobody talks."

Silence.

"What?" Connor said. "What are you looking at me for? . . . All right, nobody talks. But wait, wait," he said as we started to leave. "What about my socks?"

We looked down into the pool. "Hey," Bryce said, "you want 'em? You know how to swim."

"Very funny." We'd been concentrating so much on the bell that we hadn't noticed till now that it had gotten pretty cold. "No, really," Connor said, trailing after us through the shower room, "couldn't they, like, get my DNA off them?"[98]

---

98 Sometimes you think you know how dumb a person is, but after a while you realize that he's a whole lot dumber than that.

chapter

MISSING AIR;
SOMEBODY NEEDS A NAP;
CAR KEY

M ax."
Somebody was shaking me.
"Max!"

It was my dad. I was so-o-o-o-o asleep. . . .

"Wake up. Time to go to breakfast."

I must have mumbled something or other.

"Come on, get dressed." He laughed. "Somebody stole the bell. The counselors had to come around and get everybody up. Didn't you hear the guy yelling out there?"

"No." I curled tighter in my sleeping bag. Then . . . the bell! I poked my head out and squinted at my dad. "Somebody stole *what*?"

"The bell by the dining room."

My mom was brushing her hair. "I bet it was some counselors, playing a joke on the ones who are supposed to ring it."

"It kind of does sound like something counselors would do," my dad said. "I remember one summer when I—"

"Max, up," my mom said. "For real."

I did a lot of stumbling around the next few minutes, because I'd only gotten three or four hours' sleep. After I'd snuck back into bed, I was still so hyper that I just lay there for a long time. It was like a DVD of the whole night was playing in my head.[99]

In the dining hall the head counselor announced that the bell had been found—in the pool. Everybody laughed! Amazingly, none of us at the table looked at each other or said anything stupid.

They'd already gotten it out, the head counselor said, and he knew it was done as a prank, but the bell is the only way to communicate with the whole camp in case of emergency. Not only that, but whoever did it broke a shower-room door, and the bell had scratched up some tiles in the pool.

But that wasn't the real problem. Somebody had gone to the parking lot and let the air out of the tires of about a dozen cars. This, he said, was really dangerous, because if there was a forest fire . . .

---

99 Whenever I came to the part where Kim sat next to me in the dark, I'd hit SLOW, then REVERSE, then SLOW again. Sometimes I'd even hit PAUSE.

Huh? Somebody was out doing that while we were stealing the bell? Talk about a coincidence.

And, he said, the camp had to pay for a garage to come out and refill all the tires.

"Do you believe that?" Maddy said. "What kind of idiot? . . ."

Josh had his eyebrows up, and he was looking at Connor and Bryce and me.

"What?" Connor said.

"Oh, right," Bryce said. "As if. I wish we *had* done it."

I asked if anybody wanted to split the last pancake.

"Hey, how about coming with us on an all-day hike tomorrow?" my mom said. It was After Breakfast Cleanup Time. I was sweeping out the cabin while she folded clothes and my dad hung the unzipped sleeping bags on the clothesline to air out. "I know you've been having a good time with your friends, but it'll be our last full day here. You've got to be getting a little bored by now, and—"

I was shaking my head.

"Just listen, Max. It sounds like an amazing day. This hike goes up to a lake, too, but the trail is supposed to be more of a challenge. The counselor called it an adventure."

I sighed. "Tonight's the pizza party in town, remember? I'll probably be up really late."

My dad walked in. "You won't be up *that* late," he said. "You could still—"

"No, thanks. Really." I made a last, big sweep out

the door, leaned the broom against a wall, and threw a towel over my shoulder. "See you," I said.

At the pool four of us just happened to fall asleep for a while, lying in our usual spot, maybe twenty feet from where we'd been a few hours earlier. When one of the lifeguards came over to ask if we knew anything about the bell or the tires, Kim, Connor, Bryce, and I were still zonked out. We just blinked up at him and shook our heads and went back to sleep. Maddy and Josh were innocent, of course.

"We didn't think of doing the tires until after you went back to your cabin," Kim said later. Josh and Maddy were in the commissary, and we were sitting on the tables outside. "It was *way* cool. I wanted to hit all the cars, but we only had one air-pressure thing, and it takes longer than you think."

"Tell him the rest," Bryce said.

"You did it—you tell him," Kim said.

"Okay. Well"—Bryce looked around—"Connor and me keyed three cars. Only we used the crowbar. Way down on the bottom part of the doors, where you can't see it right away. I bet they don't even notice till they start packing up to go home. Maybe not even then." Keying a car is when you make a big, long scratch in it with a key or something.

Maddy and Josh came out with ice cream sandwiches for everybody, and Bryce shut up.

Sitting there on the table, eating my ice cream, I had to wonder what Mad Max would have done if he'd been there . . . what *I* would have done if *I'd* been there. It made me a little sick and dizzy to think about it, so I just stopped. I knew I'd been lucky to not have to decide.

Because it wasn't that long ago that I had told myself that I was never, ever, going to do anything destructive on purpose.

chapter

ENVIRONMENTAL PROTECTION; "DO IT, MAX!"; CLOUDS OF DUST

The thing is, what happened back then wasn't my fault. I mean, I didn't do it intentionally, so I didn't feel very bad about it at the time. But the more I think about it, the worse it gets. Sometimes you tell yourself that you're going to remember something the rest of your life, but usually you don't. This one I'm sure about, though.

When you go on a wilderness trail or to a park, a lot of times there are signs that say something like, "Tread softly in this place." What that means is, be careful, and watch what you're doing, because you can cause a lot of damage without meaning to. Those signs should be everywhere. And people shouldn't think they're just about harming a fragile environment, or littering.

One of the places they should put that sign is the Little League field. I told you about what a hero I was as the big guy, the star, in the minors. But I didn't tell you *all* about it.

Since I was a pitcher, between games I hung around a lot with pitchers from other teams. We'd also yell at each other during the games,[100] [101] and the better you knew the guy you were yelling at, the more fun it was.

Anyway, I kept hearing about this one kid named Lucas. For some reason he got hit almost every time he came up to bat. Practically every pitcher in the league had hit him. I wasn't pitching the first time we played his team, but our other pitcher had nailed Lucas right in the ribs.

---

100 "We want a pitcher, not a glass of water!" has to be the dumbest yell ever. It's so dumb that if friendly aliens ever listened in from one of their ships, they'd fly away and never come back. It's so dumb that if <u>unfriendly</u> aliens ever listened in from one of <u>their</u> ships, they'd instantly destroy the whole planet. I want you to know that I've never yelled, "We want a pitcher, not a glass of water!" Ever. I feel dumb just writing it. "We want a pitcher, not a belly itcher!" is pretty lame too, but at least it rhymes.

101 You should hear what girls yell at their fast-pitch softball games. I watched Sara's team one time. Some of their yells are as dumb as ours. If a pitch goes way high, they'll chant, "See the birdie? Hit the birdie. Poor birdie. Dead birdie! Birdie killer, on the mound. On the mound, BIRDIE KILLER!" But some are pretty good. When a runner steals a base, they chant, "She stole on you! She stole on you! While you were curling your hair, she was already there! She stole on you!" Or even better, "While you were pickin' your nose, she was up on her toes! She stole on you!"

I was watching a game with a couple of pitchers from other teams, and they started talking about it. "I swear I didn't mean to," said Noah, who threw left-handed. "But I heard so much about how he always got hit that I couldn't stop thinking about it. I knew he wasn't going to swing, so I wasn't throwing very hard. But I got him anyway."

"I did the same thing!" said the other pitcher, a skinny guy whose name I forget. "He goes up there all scared, like he's expecting to get hit. Then you throw it, and you hit him. It's so weird."

"And it's *so freaking funny*!" Noah said. "When I hit him, everybody on both teams cracked up. I tried not to, but I couldn't help it."

"Where'd you get him?" the skinny kid asked.

"In the back," Noah said. "Where'd you get him?"

"In the back. Half the time he's turning away before you even throw it."

"Where are *you* gonna get him?" Noah said to me.

I shook my head. "I'm not gonna get him."

The first thing I noticed about Lucas when he was waiting to come up to bat against me was that he didn't take any practice swings.[102] He just stood there

---

102 Most guys act like they're great hitters, and take superhard practice swings. You can tell they're imagining that they're hitting a home run, and that everybody's cheering. Then, when they come up to bat, they mostly just stand there and watch pitches go by, or they have really weak swings and don't even come close to the ball. That's because they're afraid they're going to get hit. And the reason they're afraid is that getting hit hurts a lot.

with the bat on his shoulder, looking scared. I'd been glancing into their dugout to see when he was coming up. When I finally saw him, I thought, *Don't worry, kid. I'm not going to hit you. I'm just going to strike you out on three pitches.*

Guys started hooting as soon as they saw him walking to the plate. They yelled to their friends at the snack bar to hurry up—Lucas is batting! In about twenty seconds the whole area behind the backstop was packed solid, with what looked like ten thousand fingers laced through the chain-link fence.

"Do it, Max!" somebody shouted.

I said to myself, "I'll do it, all right," and locked my eyes on the middle of the catcher's mitt. It was a hot day, and I was sweating. I'd been pitching for a while, so I was breathing a little hard, too. Everybody was watching me. I was in perfect control. In my whole life I'd never felt better. I gripped the ball, rocked back, then launched myself forward and fired. The ball went on a line, right down the middle of the plate and *thwack!* into the middle of the catcher's mitt. Lucas flinched and jumped back, even though the pitch hadn't come anywhere near him.

"Stee-EEEK," said the umpire.[103]

Same thing again, I told myself as the catcher threw the ball back to me. It snapped into my glove. The guys behind the backstop were chattering and laughing.

---

103 Most umpires say "Stee-EEEK" instead of "Strike." I wish I knew why.

Lucas held the bat up, but he was so scared that it was kind of wobbling. Same thing again: I stared at the catcher's mitt, gripped the ball, rocked back, launched myself forward, and fired, exactly as I'd done before, exactly as I always did, and the ball zoomed away like it was on an invisible track that cut through the air and led straight to Lucas's face.

He spun away and threw his left arm up. The ball hit him smack on the elbow, and the *crack!* it made was so loud that the kids behind the backstop, the parents in the stands, and all the players on both teams were so quiet so fast that you could hear the *thump!* when Lucas hit the ground. He landed on his right side. Puffs of dust rose up around him. Then he was rolling around in the dirt, holding his arm and crying. His coach came out from their dugout, moving in that slow coach-trot that they all know how to do.

Now I could hear the guys behind the screen.

"Whoa!"

"You see that?"

"Whoa!"

The coach was bending over Lucas, his hands on his knees, talking to him. The coach was wearing a red baseball cap and sunglasses, so I couldn't see much of his face, but he acted like he'd done this a lot. I couldn't make out what he was saying at first, but after a minute he was talking a little louder.

"Come on now, son," he said. "You're all right. Come on." He helped Lucas up and brushed him off. *Big* clouds of dust. Then he patted him on the helmet, gave an "Okay" nod to the umpire, and coach-trotted back to the dugout.

Lucas walked slowly to first base, still rubbing his elbow. His face was coated with dirt, except for two tracks washed clean by tears. He never even looked at me.

I told myself not to feel guilty. Hey, it was an accident, and this is baseball.

My parents got to the game late, and hadn't seen it happen. When I told them about it in the car on the way home, they both started talking at the same time.

"That's so sad!" my mom said, just as my dad was saying, "What a great story!"

She looked at him. *"What?"*

"I mean, of course it's sad," my dad said. "But you have to admit—"

"It's just *heartbreaking*," my mom said. "That poor child. I wonder why he keeps playing."

"And you tried *not* to hit him," my dad said. "I have to tell you, stuff like that happens sometimes. Not that you're going to hit people with baseballs, but—"

"I get it," I said. By then I couldn't wait to be by myself. When we got home, I went straight to my room, closed the door, and froze. Then I said, "Sometimes you try to tread softly, and you end up stomping on something anyway." It was like I didn't really understand it until I said it out loud.

EXTREME PING-PONG; SAD FACE; PIZZA WITH EVERYTHING

That afternoon we all went to my cabin because my parents were supposed to be at some crafts class. We got there just as the camp doctor was leaving.

"Whichever one of you has a father in there," she said, "now has a father with a sprained ankle. He's okay, but he won't be getting around much for a while."

I rushed in. My dad was lying on the cot with his left foot propped up on a couple of pillows, an ice pack around his ankle, and a damp washcloth over his eyes. A pair of crutches leaned in the corner.

"You have before you the first person in the history of the world to sprain an ankle playing Ping-Pong," my mom said as everybody crowded into the cabin to take a look. She was bringing my dad a cup of water and a couple of pills. "Okay, babe, sit up."

He took off the washcloth and struggled up on

his elbows. "What she's not telling you," he said, "is that I made the shot."[104] He took the pills and handed the cup back to her. Then he looked around at all of us. "Okay," he said. "Showtime." He leaned forward. "Slowly," he mumbled as he lifted off the ice pack. "Easy . . . Ow! . . . Easy . . ."

We crowded around. His ankle was so swollen, it didn't even look real.

"Awesome!" Connor said. "Does it hurt?"

Josh gave him a soft slap on the side of the head, something I'd never seen him do—Connor was always the one slapping people. "Yes, Connor," Josh said, "I think it probably hurts."

On their way out everybody said, "Hope you feel better," "Yeah," "Feel better," "Sorry it happened," that stuff.

"Thanks," my dad said. "But look at the size of that thing! It's quite an accomplishment, don't you think?"

Maddy saw me roll my eyes. She leaned toward me and said, "Remember, crazy is good."

My mom gave me a look that said "Hang around," so I hung around and played gin rummy with my dad. When I was little, he used to let me win. Not anymore.

"So much for tomorrow's hike," he said. "Discard."

"I discarded the seven," I said.

---

104 Later some guys told me what he yelled when he sprained his ankle. "No, and I'm surprised you even repeated those words to me," my mom said when I asked her if I could put it in the book.

He looked down. "Oh, right." He picked it up. "But you go," he said to my mom. "Unless you want to sit around all day and listen to me complain."

"Tough choice," she said. "I'll think about it."

"Discard," I said.

"Max," she said, "want to take his place? Keep me company?"

"Mom—"

"Okay, okay," my mom said. "It was just a suggestion."

"Gin," my dad said, and laid his cards on the bed.

"What?" I said. "How? . . ."

That evening about thirty of us crammed into four big vans for the trip to the pizza place. My friends and I picked the one Camille was driving.

"How'd I get so lucky?" she said when she saw us piling in. Then she said, "Your regular orange headband, Max? This isn't a fancy enough occasion for the blue one?"

"Nah," I said. "It's just pizza."

"Let's go to a sushi place instead," Kim said. I'd tried to sit next to her, but Bryce had gotten there first.

"I vote for burgers," Bryce said.

"Mexican," I said.

Josh: "Italian."

Connor: "Burgers."

Maddy: "Vegetarian."

All the rest of us: "No-o-o-o-o!"

"Well, I'm driving to the pizza place," Camille said as she started guiding the van along the crunchy dirt road. "If you want to try to order sushi or Mexican or hamburgers or whatever, good luck."

The restaurant had a whole room in back reserved for us. "Let's not sit with Maddy," Kim whispered to me as we walked in. "She'll want a crappy vegetarian pizza."

"Okay," I whispered back. "Let's take that table over . . . *there*!" I made a dash for it. Kim was right behind me, and Bryce and Connor right behind her. It was a table for four, so that was that. Maddy and Josh ended up sitting with Camille and another counselor, at a table so close behind us that I had to scoot my chair up so Maddy and Camille could get in.

"I'd like to see the sushi menu, please," Kim said when the waitress came around. She was about nineteen or twenty, and looked kind of worn-out. She had long brown hair tied back in a ponytail, but some strands had come loose and were falling across her face.

"What?" she said. She was trying to comb her hair back with her fingers. "I didn't catch that."

"Never mind," Kim said.

"Sorry," the waitress said. "Long day."

"Sad face," Kim said.

"I'm sorry—what?" the waitress said.

"Never *mind*," Kim said. "Jeez."

"I can't stand stupid waitresses," Kim said after we'd ordered our stuff. "Just watch. She'll mess everything up."

The pizza took a long time. "The whole room ordered at once," the waitress said when we asked about it, "and the kitchen got a little behind. I'll bring it out as soon as it's ready."

"Aren't you *supposed* to bring it out as soon as it's ready?" Kim said.

Some of the loose strands of hair were stuck to the waitress's sweaty forehead. She started to say something but changed her mind. Then she looked right at Kim and said, "Yes. You're exactly right. I'm supposed to bring it out as soon as it's ready," and walked away.

"God, what an idiot," Kim said.

"If she lost twenty pounds, she wouldn't miss any of them," Bryce said.

We all laughed. Connor said, "Make that twenty-five pounds," and we laughed louder.

"I think we should stiff her," Kim said.

"Yeah!" Bryce said. I didn't know what that meant, but I figured that Mad Max would, so I didn't ask. But Connor did.

"That's when you don't leave a tip," Kim told him. "And she doesn't deserve one." The camp was paying for the pizzas, but we'd been told the tip was up to us. My mom had given me two dollars.

"So Fatso gets zero," Bryce said.

"Fatso gets zero," Kim said.

I could feel the two bills I'd tucked into my right front pocket.

When we got up to leave, nobody had put any money on the table. I knew I should, but I didn't want Kim to see me doing it. As we were going out the door, I looked back and saw the waitress clearing the table.

She must have known by then that we didn't leave her anything, but I couldn't see her face.

We went out to the van. Camille was already in the driver's seat, and Josh was sitting inside, but Maddy was standing by the open sliding door.

"Why don't you guys take one of the other vans?" she said.

Connor said, "What's your big pain-in-the-ass problem?"

"Not my problem at all," Maddy said. "You're the ones that have a problem."

Kim said, "Right. Whatever. I don't like the smell in this van anyway." She and Connor and Bryce walked away. "She's such a bitch," I heard her say. Maddy heard it too.

I looked at Maddy and kind of spread my arms. "What? . . ." I said.

She was only a few feet away, but she took two steps forward, so she was right in my face.

"We heard what happened in there with that waitress," she said. "You just *do not treat people that way.*" Her voice was shaking, she was so mad. "It's not *right.* It makes me *sick.* And *you* make me sick. Does that explain it well enough for you?"

"But I didn't—" I said, but she had already turned and was climbing into the van. Kim, Connor, and Bryce were laughing about something as they got into another one. Maddy reached forward in her seat and slammed the door shut. So I was standing there alone in the dark parking lot.

Okay, Mad Max, I said to myself. *NOW what are you going to do?*

I looked over at the other van, then back at this one. Maddy and Josh and Camille were just shadows inside. Then I said, softly but out loud, "Mad Max isn't going to do anything, but *I* am." I grabbed the handle and slid the door open again.

"Next van," Josh said. "Plenty of room over there."

"I like this one," I said, and moved past the two of them to the very back. Some older guys climbed in and took the rest of the seats. They talked all the way back to camp. Not a word from Maddy. Or Josh. Or Camille. Or me.

I expected my parents to be asleep, but they were both up because my dad's ankle was hurting him so much.

"Still going on that hike tomorrow?" I asked my mom.

15

chapter

1, 2, 3, HIKE!;
GOOD-BYE #1;
GOOD-BYE #2

T hat was the best hike I've ever been on, maybe the best hike I ever *will* be on. It was good for so many reasons that I had to make a list.

1) It got me out of camp for the whole day. I didn't even want to see any of the people I'd been with practically 16/5.

2) It gave me time to think.

3) It felt good to get completely exhausted.

4) It was a great day with my mom, who treated me like I was her hiking partner and never once told me what to do.

5) The lake was *incredible*.

We made it back in time for dinner, but just barely. My dad was getting around okay on his crutches,[105] so we all went to the dining hall, and sat down at a table together. I saw Josh and Maddy sitting with all their parents and Maddy's little sisters. Kim, Connor, and Bryce were at our old table, way in the back, with some of the guys who'd gone to the pizza place.

The counselors put on a farewell campfire show that night. I didn't say anything about it to my parents—just walked down with them and sat with them on a big log. Maddy and Josh were there too. I caught Maddy's eye and started to wave to her, but she looked away.

Everybody was supposed to be out of the camp by ten the next morning. Since my dad couldn't do much, my mom and I did most of the packing. It looked like we weren't going to have time to go to breakfast, so I went to the dining hall to get some food to bring back to the cabin. Just as I stepped up onto the porch, Connor and Bryce came out.

"Mad Max!" they said together, almost like they'd practiced it.

Connor tried to slap me on the side of the head, but I was ready for him and knocked his arm away. He laughed. "You coming back next year, bro?"

"Probably not. How about you?"

"I'm gonna tell my parents I'm getting too old for

---

105 I tried them out, but they were way too big for me. It's amazing how much fun it is to pretend that you're hurt, and how much fun it's _not_ to actually be hurt.

this," he said. "Bryce here's going to have to survive without me."

"Hey, I'm done with this place," Bryce said.

The screen door slammed. "You won't see me back at this jacked-up baby camp." That was Kim, who'd just walked out. "And you won't see me at all in about five minutes, because we're outta here." She hugged Bryce, then Connor, then me. "Bye, Maximillian," she whispered. I didn't hug her back, but I don't think she noticed. "You guys made it tolerable, at least," she said. She walked down the steps and waved without turning around. "See ya," she called out, "but probably not."

When we had everything in the car, I told my parents I'd be back in a few minutes.

Things looked frantic at Maddy and Josh's cabins—car doors and trunks open, people carrying boxes and sleeping bags, Maddy's sisters running around. Josh saw me and acted like he didn't. Maddy came out of her cabin carrying a couple of full laundry bags. I walked right up to her before she had a chance to ignore me.

"Those other guys are jerks," I said. "I'm not a jerk. I just wanted to tell you."

She shifted the laundry bags around in her arms. "Who says you're not a jerk?"

"I do," I said. "Really, I'm not. And I didn't say anything to that waitress."

"You went along with it, didn't you?"

"No. I mean, I didn't *mean* to, but . . . okay, I acted like a jerk. But that doesn't mean I am one. Most of the time I'm not, anyway."

Maddy put the laundry bags down. Her mother was walking by us on the way into the cabin. She stopped, like she was going to say something, but after she glanced at Maddy, she just went on in.

"Did you guys steal the bell and let the air out of those tires?" Maddy said. "Josh thinks you did. He said that some of the counselors think so too."

I was instantly chilled inside, but I was pretty sure it didn't show. *"What?"* I said, and kind of laughed. "No! Get real." I jammed my hands into my pockets and looked around, then back at her. "Anyway, are you guys coming back next year?"

That surprised her. She blinked a couple of times. "We were talking about it. Maybe. Why—are you?"

I took off my headband and started twirling it around my finger. "Same thing," I said. "Maybe."

"Well," she said. "I guess if you do, and if we do, then I'll see you then, right?"

"Right," I said, and let the headband fly. It went straight up and got itself caught on a pine branch. Maddy and I looked at it, then back at each other. "Oh," I said, "and can you tell Josh I'm not a jerk?"

"I'm still not sure about that."

"Well, tell him I might not be as big a jerk as you thought I was."

"Okay. That's fair. Anything else?"

"Yeah. Do you text?"

She tried not to smile, but finally she did. "Everybody texts," she said.

Part Three
Dancing

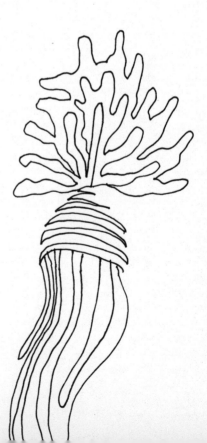

chapter

MAD MAX

I t took more than a hundred miles, all the way down that twisty mountain road and maybe an hour on the freeway heading home, before I finally admitted to myself why I felt sick when I thought about those guys letting the air out of tires and keying those cars. It was because I knew that even though I would never have done those things, I wouldn't have tried to stop Connor and Bryce. I couldn't have, and still been Mad Max. And I *wouldn't* have—not with Kim there.

Just as bad, maybe worse, was that I'd lied to Maddy's face.[106] I didn't feel too good about that, either.

---

106 I asked my mom what's the difference between lying to somebody and lying to somebody's face. She said they mean the same thing, but when you say you lied to somebody's face, it sounds more personal—you deliberately told a lie to someone who trusted you. But another part of the meaning must be that I can still see Maddy's face as I stood there and lied to her.

It had been so amazing to be wild and unpredictable, loud and out-there and a little crazy. But I ended up spending a lot of time with people I didn't like very much, and the people I did like thought I was a jerk.[107]

But I didn't want to go back to just being the old Max, because as Mad Max, I could make myself do things that I was too shy, or too scared, or just too *little* to do before.

And anyway, Mad Max wasn't some made-up, make-believe person. Parts of him really *were* me. I just had to find out which parts fit and which parts didn't. There's a saying that goes, "To thine own self be true."[108] But before I could be true to my own self, I had to figure out who my own self was.

Anyway, Mad Max was coming home with me. And it turned out that I'd have to figure out how to deal with him on the same night I sat on the plate of spaghetti.

---

[107] Are you as tired of that word as I am? I'm going to try to stop using it.

[108] I got that from my dad. He said it's from <u>Hamlet</u>, the Shakespeare play. If you're writing a book report on <u>Anyway*</u>, be sure to include that quote, because teachers love it when you use Shakespeare. It'll turn a B into a B+, or a B+ into an A-. Guaranteed.

chapter

NO PARKING;
PARTY POOPERS;
NOT-SO-MAD MAX

T he plan was for us to stop at another motel that
night. On the drive up to camp, while I had been
creating Mad Max[109] in my head, it seemed like
my parents had talked about every motel we passed.

"We could stay there on the way back."

"That one's way too close to the freeway."

"Look! Free breakfast!"

But when my dad starts driving, he doesn't want to
stop. It turned out that was true even though he had a
bad ankle. When my mom said, "We could stay at the
same place we stayed at on the way up," he said he felt
like driving all the way.

"We'll wake up in our own beds tomorrow morning and have the whole day," he said. "And we won't
have to pay for a motel."

---

109 That wasn't my name yet, of course.

So no private room for me. I didn't argue because I knew it wouldn't be any use. My mom knew it too. All she said was, "Well, let's take some of that motel money and stop at a nice place for dinner, and take our time. It's going to be a long enough trip, and I don't want to get home all frazzled and exhausted."

"Sounds good," my dad said. "Hey, call Ben. He's not expecting us till tomorrow."

She fished out her cell. "He's not answering," she said. "I'll leave a message."

"Nah," my dad said. "Let's surprise him."

And we did.

"What's with all the cars?" my dad said. It was almost ten, and we were two blocks from home. Cars were parked solid on both sides of the street.

"Somebody's having a party," my mom said.[110]

We found out who was having the party when we couldn't get into our driveway because there were two cars parked in it. All the lights in the house were on, music was blasting, the front door was open, and there were people standing in the doorway holding bottles of what I was sure was beer.

"What the hell?" my dad said.

---

110 That's now a famous line in our family. We say it whenever we see a lot of cars. It doesn't matter where. It can be a mall parking lot, or a traffic jam on the freeway, even a new-car showroom. One of us will say, "Somebody's having a party." One of us besides Ben, that is. All Ben will say is, "Very funny."

"What the *hell*?" my mom said.

I figured it was safe for me to say "What the hell?" too, so I did.

My dad pulled into the Oshimas' driveway next door. Mr. Oshima came right out of his house, yelling, "Hey! You can't park—" Then he saw it was us.

"Oh, hi," he said. He looked over at our house. "I should have known you guys weren't home. Ben's having a party, huh?"

"Not for long," my dad said. "I'll move the car in a few minutes."

"No rush," Mr. Oshima said. He was still looking at our house. "Need any help?"

My dad was getting out of the car, kind of hopping to stay off his bad ankle. He started to say no. Then he thought about it for a couple of seconds and said, "Sure. Come on, let's clear the place out."

I got his crutches from the backseat and handed them to him. My mom was already stepping up onto the porch. She grabbed beer bottles out of the hands of the two guys and a girl in the doorway. "Party's over," she said, and walked on in.

One of the guys said, "Who does that babe[III] think she is?"

"That babe is Ben's mother," my dad said as he crutched his way up to the house. "I'm Ben's father. Got any more questions?"

III The next day I told her what that guy had said. "He did not!" she said. "Did he?"

The other guy said, "Who's Ben?" His friends pulled him off the porch, and they took off across the front yard.

We stepped inside. "Max," my dad yelled, "find out where the music's coming from, and turn it off!" I was right next to him, but I could barely hear him. The music was so loud, it seemed to be coming from everywhere. I waded into a living room full of people I'd never seen before. Most of them were about Ben's age, but some didn't look much older than me. I felt my foot go *squish* on the carpet, and I looked down and found out why the whole house smelled like beer. There were bottles and cans on the floor, and on every table, and on the arms of every chair. I took another step. *Squish*, went my other foot. I couldn't hear it, but I could sure feel it.

I said to myself, *Ben's going to be on Electronic Restriction forever. And we don't even* have *Electronic Restriction.*

But it was incredibly exciting. My mom and dad and Mr. Oshima and I were going to throw all these people out of the house! And I'd been given an important assignment: *Stop the music.*

A huge boom box was sitting on the dining room table. The problem: two very big guys, both wearing torn and faded black T-shirts with lists of the cities some band had played in written on the backs. Different bands, but the shirts looked about the same. The two Music Monsters were standing over the boom box, shuffling through CDs and shouting at each other, probably about what to play next.

I turned around to look for my dad. But I stopped and turned back.

"Mad Max," I whispered.

A thrilling rush filled my chest, because I *knew* I was going to do it. Then I did. I squish-squished over and yanked the cord out of the wall.

It was suddenly dead silent. The Music Monsters looked around and couldn't believe what they were seeing, which was me, standing there with the cord in my hand. People started going, "Hey!" and "MUSIC! MUUUUUUUUUSIC!"

One of the Music Monsters shouted, "You little twerp, what do you think you're—"

"PARTY'S OVER! EVERYBODY OUT! PARTY'S OVER! EVERYBODY OUT!"

That was my mom, clapping her hands and walking from room to room. I guess most of these people had moms, and recognized that tone of voice, because a whole lot of them, from all over the house, headed for the door. Even the two Music Monsters were leaving, one carrying the boom box, the other a stack of CDs. All they did was give me a dirty look. *Oooooh*, that hurt so bad.

But some party animals didn't seem to hear my mom, or they just ignored her, because ten or fifteen of them were still standing around, drinking beer and talking. I saw my dad moving two guys toward the front door by herding them with his crutches. Mr. Oshima was right behind him, holding another guy by the back of his collar. The guy didn't look too happy about it, but he didn't struggle or fight or anything. Mr. Oshima passed him to my dad, who swept him out the door with one of his crutches. My mom was kind of escorting two girls, holding each one by the upper arm. She waited until my dad moved Mr. Oshima's guy out, then walked the girls out the door.

"Good night, ladies," she said. Then she came back into the house to get some more. Mad Max came up with the brilliant idea that maybe *I* could throw one of those guys out, but I told him to shut up.

We found Ben in the backyard, sitting on a lawn chair. He looked like he was half-asleep, but there were empty beer cans lying around, so that wasn't it. He didn't realize that we were standing there. My dad took one of his crutches and poked him in the ribs. He looked up. Then he moaned, "Oh no," and leaned forward and put his head in his hands.

"Benjamin," my mom said, "what—"

"I just invited a few guys over," he said. "Really. That's all. But it got crazy." He was kind of whining and moaning at the same time. "People just kept coming and coming and coming and coming. I told them to leave, but nobody would listen to me."

"So you decided to see how much beer you could drink," she said.

Ben started to answer. Then he was quiet. Then he threw up on the grass.

"Max," my mom said, "go to bed."

Early the next morning the sounds of clinking and clanking woke me up. I went into the living room and saw Ben dragging around a big black garbage bag, picking up bottles and cans, and tossing them in. He looked like he'd slept in his clothes. His hair was sticking out all over the place. Sometimes when a bottle or a can clinked or clanked, he'd close his eyes tight.

"You should have everything pretty much cleaned up in a few hours. Then you can go to the hardware store and rent a rug shampooer." That was my mom. I hadn't seen my dad and her standing there. They were in their robes. My dad didn't have his crutches, so he was kind of leaning on her.

"Remember to buy rug shampoo," my dad said. "Oh, and I told Mr. Oshima you'd mow his lawn this afternoon."

My mom noticed me. "Hi, sweetie," she said. "You sleep okay?"

"Yeah, sure," I said. I squished into the kitchen and poured myself some orange juice and listened to Ben cleaning up. I guessed that the This Is Dumb software in his brain needed upgrading, and that my parents had decided to step in and do the tech work.

chapter

ALICE; ALL ALICE; NO, REALLY, THIS CHAPTER IS JUST—WELL, MOSTLY— ABOUT ALICE

I've been putting this off, but now I think it's time to tell you about what I did to Alice.

It happened a few years ago, long before very much of *my* This Is Dumb software had been installed. It could have also been an early lesson for me about Treading Softly, but I was only nine years old and didn't have any brains at all.

This is another baseball story, kind of. Remember what I said about how when kids are waiting to come up to bat, they take all these hard, tough-looking practice swings and pretend that they're hitting home runs, and that everybody's cheering? Well, the way I know that is because when I take practice swings, I pretend exactly the same thing.[112] And one afternoon

---

112 And just like most other guys, when I actually come up to bat, I have a pretty weak swing because I'm so afraid the pitch is going to hit me. I really, really wish that weren't true, but it is.

after school I took a bat into our backyard and started swinging away, hitting imaginary home run after home run after home run. *Bam! Bam! Bam! Bam!*

Crack.

Alice had come bounding up from behind me. I knew she was in the yard, but I just wasn't paying attention. I had swung as hard as I could, and the bat caught her on the side of her head. She gave a little yelp as she flipped over in the air. She landed solidly on her side and just lay there, her eyes wide open. Blood ran from her mouth.

I dropped the bat.

"NO-O-O-O-O-O-O-O!" I screamed. Then I was on my knees, crying. "Alice! Alice! *NO-O-O-O!*"

The back door flew open and Ben came running out. He knelt down beside her, his hand on her chest. "I can't even tell if she's breathing," he said. "We've got to get her to the vet." He ran back inside to call our mom and dad.

"Alice!" I was crying hysterically. "Alice! ALICE!"

I don't remember what happened in the next few minutes, but I found myself running down the street to get to my parents' car sooner. That didn't make any sense, but that's what I was doing. As they came driving up, I waved my arms frantically. They stopped, and I got in.

"I think Alice is dead! I killed her!"

"Just hang on," my mom said.

When the car got in the driveway, we jumped out so fast that we left all the doors open. I bolted through the house, with my mom and dad right behind me. We ran into the backyard and saw . . .

Alice. Sitting in a lawn chair.[113] Ben was petting her softly. She was shaking a little, and her brown-and-white chest had flecks of red on it from the blood that dripped from her jaw.

But she was sitting there. Alive.

That was, and still is, the best, most wonderful thing I've seen in my whole entire life. Because I knew, I just *knew* that I had killed my dog, and that I'd never, ever, *ever* get over it. Yet there she was.

I walked over very slowly and put my arms around her. She licked my ear with her warm, wet doggie tongue, like she always does. And I laughed, like I always do.

"A few minutes ago," Ben said, "she gave this little jerk[114] and sat up. Then she jumped up on the chair. She must have just been stunned. I think she's all right."

"Well, not quite," my dad said, looking closely at her bloody jaw.

The vet told us that I had knocked out a tooth and cracked another one. A couple of weeks later, after Alice had completely recovered from the blow to her head, we took her in to have the cracked tooth removed. To do that, the vet had to knock her out,

---

113 I'm pretty sure this was the same lawn chair we'd find Ben in three years later.

114 This is a different kind of "jerk," so it doesn't count.

and I surprised myself by starting to cry all over again. But that's something I've gotten used to, because I choke up every time[115] I think about what happened. And every time I think about what *almost* happened.

For a long time I tried not to think about it at all. But lately, with all that's been going on, the Alice accident seems more and more important.

There was no good reason why Alice wasn't killed, or hurt so badly that there'd have been something wrong with her for the rest of her life. It was just good luck that I hit her in a place in the head where it didn't do too much damage. If I had hit her a few inches higher up, it would have been right in the eye. A few inches lower, and it could have crushed her throat.

Although I didn't realize it at the time, this was my first real example of how anything can happen, and for no reason, and that everything can go terribly wrong in an instant. Mostly, of course, it doesn't. You accidentally stab somebody with a pencil, and he's okay, no big deal. You hit a kid with a baseball, and you hurt him a little, but he's all right. You bash your dog in the head with a bat, and a few minutes later she's sitting up.

But you're not going to be that lucky all the time, forever.

That's why it's important to tread softly, and why

---

[115] Like now, for example.

I had to watch myself, to be careful about what I did as Mad Max. We cause enough harm just by accident, without going around looking for ways to make bad things happen. Sometimes you end up stomping on something anyway.

DON'T SAY "CHEESE!";
DOUBLE PLAY;
LAWN CHAIR THREAT

We were back from camp a couple of weeks before Sara's party. Her idea of having Evan and me on her planning committee went away after the 16-Ounce-Suicide Disaster, and I wasn't going to remind her. In fact, I was going to avoid her, which should have been easy because we weren't in school.

There was one close call, though. A few days after we got back, I was in the little secret room in the front window of the store, dusting and organizing spare body parts, when I heard a familiar voice from just on the other side of the wall. It was Sara, talking with my mom like they were old friends. They went on and on and on. I carefully, quietly moved some arms out of the way to make a space for myself, and sat down. Mannequins were standing over me like I was in a really strange forest.

The room was warm. Before, I was always cramped

and uncomfortable in there, but that day, down on the floor, it was like I fit in perfectly. The voices slowly became a buzzing drone, and I let myself drift away.

Then the secret door was open, and my mom was looking down at me. "It's safe," she said. "No classmates in the immediate vicinity."

"Um," I ummed, trying to figure out where I was.

"Max, don't move," she said. She was tilting her head to one side, then the other, which can mean only one thing. "I love the way you're sitting with all those arms, and you're surrounded by all those legs. I'm going to get my camera." [116]

"Mom—"

"Don't. You. MOVE!" So I didn't. I know the rules. I've been in this family a long time.

Since it was summer, I had to work every Saturday, unless there was a Little League game. And no more minor league for me. I wasn't a star anymore, but that was okay. In a way, it was fun just to be a regular player again.

Anyway, I told you Wiley McNaught would get me back for what I did to him in Macy's. And when we played his team, he found a really, really good way. At least, that's what I thought he was doing.

I was playing second base. McNaught was on first after hitting a single. The next guy up hit a two-hopper to the shortstop. McNaught took off, running hard from

---

116 My mom refuses to take normal, ordinary pictures, and my dad never takes any pictures at all. Everybody thinks their own family is weird, but I have photographic proof.

first base, straight at me. It was my job to catch the throw from the shortstop, step on second base, and turn and throw it to first. It was McNaught's job to stop me from doing that.

I caught the ball.

I stepped on second.

I turned to throw to first.

McNaught blasted me halfway into left field.

The shortstop told me later that it looked like we were playing football, and McNaught had put a perfect block on a linebacker. What he did was completely fair: He was a baserunner, and I was in his way. He was out, of course, since I'd stepped on the base before he got there. After the play was over, he dusted himself off and trotted toward his team's dugout. He passed me as the shortstop was helping me up off the ground.

"How does it feel?" McNaught said to me as he went by. "Huh? How does it *feel*?"

I squinted up at him. "What?"

He just laughed.

That was on a Wednesday afternoon, and on Friday I still hurt. Evan was spending a week with us while his parents were off on vacation. His little sister was with an aunt or something. Their parents had gone to a resort in Mexico. They'd told Evan he could come along.

"But I could tell they didn't want me to," he said. "They kept saying, 'Well, you can go to the pool, and there's cable TV.'"

We were sitting around in my room after dinner when I got yet another brilliant idea. Evan's parents were always ditching him, and my parents went to that family camp mostly for me. So—what if Evan came to camp with us next year? I'd told him all about it,[17] and he'd been especially interested in the parts about 1) the great hike to the lake, 2) the picnic tables loaded with food, and 3) Maddy. Hmmm. Maybe this wasn't such a good idea.

Just kidding. And I knew it'd be okay with my parents, because one time I overheard them talking about how Evan is such a good influence.[118]

Evan said, "Yeah! My parents would love to get rid of me for a week next summer too. They'd probably pay you guys double what the camp costs."

"That's perfect," I said. "We can use the extra

---

17 Well, about _most_ of it. I left out the part about how I made myself into Mad Max. Evan is _my_ best friend and all, but I wanted to keep that to myself.

118 Sometimes I wonder why Evan is still friends with me, when he does just about everything so much better than I do, and could hang out with anybody. One time I asked him, in a kidding way so he wouldn't know that I really meant it. We were playing burn-out, which is a baseball game of catch—only you throw the ball as hard as you can. Usually one guy just stops because the other guy is throwing too hard for him to handle it. Whenever Evan and I play burn-out, I'm the one who stops. Every time. But he knew it was a serious question. He caught my throw, then held on to the ball. "Because you're funny," he said. "And you're weird. In a good way, I mean. I'm so dull, I bore myself. Sometimes I wonder why _you_ hang out with _me_."

"So do I," I said.

"See?" he said. "Funny." Then he burned me out.

money to hit the commissary five times a day." This was *so* going to happen. I'd been texting Maddy every couple of days since we got back from camp, and I'd pretty much convinced her that I wasn't really a (not-going-to-use-that-word-again). So when I sent her the idea about Evan, she texted right back. Evan grabbed my phone and sent her a message, and she started texting Josh, and after half an hour we practically had the whole week of next summer's camp planned out.

It had been a hot day, and it was still hot in the house, so we went out into the backyard to sit in lawn chairs and cool off and look at the sky. Alice came with us. She made a little groaning sound as she lay down, the way she always does, but it wasn't as loud as the groaning sound I made as I sat down. McNaught had nailed me pretty good.

"You'll be out of intensive care by next Saturday," Evan said. That was Sara's party.

"Good," I said. "I'll be able to dance without groaning. Girls don't like it if you groan a lot when you're dancing. They can't hear the music."

After about a minute Evan said, "Shooting star," and pointed.

A few seconds later I said, "Shooting star," and pointed to a different part of the sky.

After about another minute I said, "I might not be groaning, but that doesn't mean I'll be able to dance."

The closer it got to the party, the more I was worrying. I remembered that Sara said that Allie was nervous about it, and I kind of wanted to call Allie. But I

knew I wasn't going to, or even text her. I'd been trying to get Mad Max to do it, but since I'd come home
and everything was back to normal, he was hiding or
something.

"Hardly anybody's going to know how to really
dance," Evan said. He closed his eyes and leaned back
in his chair.[119] "They're all going to be faking it. Just
watch everybody else, and do what they're doing.
Nobody'll notice, and nobody'll care."

Here I was freaking out, and Evan seemed completely relaxed about the whole thing. I remembered
how all of a sudden I had thought that Aaron Krugman was so immature, and how I had never called
him again. Now Evan was handling this party thing
like he was a lot older than me. And I was *feeling* like
he was a lot older than me.

That gave me something else to worry about. What
if Evan started looking at me like *I* was a little kid?

Wherever Mad Max was, I needed him back. Soon.

---

119   He was sitting in the famous Alice-and-Ben
chair. Isn't it strange how it keeps sneaking
into the story?

BEN THE EXPERT;
MISSING PERSONS;
PROBLEM

B en had some advice for me as I was getting ready to go to the party. He put his hands on either side of the bathroom doorway and leaned in. I was looking at myself in the mirror and trying to decide whether Mad Max would come back if I wore a headband.

"Take it from me, and go easy on the beer," he said. "Four or five max, Max."

Guess who happened to be passing by in the hall. "Ben, that's not—"

"Oh, come on. He knows I'm kidding."

"Yeah," I said. "And anyway, I hardly ever have more than three."

"As I was *going* to say," my mom said, "that's not funny. Max, you have to promise me, if there's *any*—"

"Mom," I said, "where is this party?"

"Sara's house," she said. "Okay, I get the—"

"You know Sara, right? And you know her parents?"

"Sometimes kids bring—"

"Do you have any idea what Sara would do to some-body who brought beer or something to her party? Do you?"

My mom sighed. "Max, you told me yourself it was going to be a big party, and that you don't even like some of the kids who are going be there. Like that boy, what's his—"

"McNaught."

"Whoa!" Ben said. "The guy who hammered you on that double-play ball?"

"Yeah, Sara's mom is friends with his mom or something."

"Well," Ben said, "just don't ask him to dance, and you should be okay."

"Ben," my mom said, "you're not helping. No, seri-ously, Max, if—"

"Mom."

"If any—"

"Mom."

"Okay, I'll stop." She walked away, then came right back. "But if any—"

"Mom!"

I had gotten there a little late because it took me so long to decide yes or no about the headband.[120] Mrs. Chen led me through the house, past Sara's younger brother Alex's room. Alex was in there with one of his

---

120 No.

friends. Sara had told me they were under orders to stay away from us. "And they will," she said, "because Alex knows if they don't, I'll kill him."

Music was coming from the backyard. Mrs. Chen pointed down the hall in that direction. "Party's out there," she said. "I bet you can find it."

One thing about Sara's house is that it has this huge backyard. They had rented a dance floor, a wooden platform that was set up right in the middle of the yard. Nobody was on it yet. There were white folding chairs all over the place, and two long tables with sodas and chips were set up by the wall of the garage. It was still light out, but the floodlights were starting to make a difference.[121]

I recognized a couple of girls from the fast-pitch softball game I'd watched,[122] and a lot of people from

---

[121] That's my favorite time of day, or night, or whatever you want to call it. Dusk, I guess. (No way will I ever use the word "twilight.") The light looks different. Everything's in-between and changing—you feel like something is about to happen. It's especially true in summer, maybe because you're outside more, or because it's suddenly not as hot, and there's more energy in the air. That's sure how it felt at Sara's party, anyway.

[122] "She stole on you! She stole on you! While you were pickin' your nose, she was up on her toes! She stole on you!" Sorry. I just wanted to get that in one more time.

school, but I had no idea who some of the others were. That made me instantly more nervous than I already was. I headed over to the tables to get a soda, just so I'd be doing *something*. I fished a can of lemon-lime out of a cooler and looked around for somebody to talk to.

Evan was over on the far side of the yard, next to the table with the boom box. He was with the two softball girls. I pictured myself wearing the headband at camp, walking along the edge of the pool and then just plunking myself down with five people I didn't know. I saw myself lifting the bell, yanking the cord out of the wall. *Try to remember how that felt,* I half whispered. *Try to remember.*

Well, one of the things about Mad Max is that he doesn't think everything to death. He acts, he moves. So I told myself to just walk over there. Just start walking. So I did. I started—

"Max."

It was Sara. "Oh, hey," I said. "Cool dance floor."

"Allie's not here."

I shrugged. "She'll get here," I said. "I just got here myself."

"No, I mean, she's not coming."

"What? Why not?"

Sara frowned. "She called a little while ago. She said she was too nervous, and it was making her sick. So I told her it was okay if she didn't come."

I tried to think of the right thing to say. "Well," I said, "it's not like it's going to ruin your party or anything. There's all these people already here, and—"

She started to slug me in the arm. I flinched. But she stopped, like it wasn't worth the trouble.

"You moron," she said. "I'm not worried about my *party*. I'm worried about *Allie*."

"Oh. Right."

"Would you call her?" She waved at some people who must've been waving at her. "Ask her how she's doing? Try to make her feel better?"

"You mean, call her now?"

"Yes, now. What, are you busy?"

"Why do you want *me* to call her?"

"You know what? You really *are* a moron. Why do you think she's been so nervous?"

"I don't know. Party?"

"Yeah, right. Party. Party with *you* here."

"What? Oh . . . *what*?" The idea that I could make a girl nervous was ridiculous. I mean, I'm just me.

"Max, that thing that happened at the mall made her really shy around boys. I mean, even shyer than she used to be. Especially around you." Sara was talking even slower and more evenly than she usually does. I felt like I'd been hit by a freeze ray—I couldn't even blink. "She's home feeling terrible, and I think you should talk to her. Have you got your cell?"

"Huh?" Things were happening so fast that I wasn't exactly thinking clearly. "Oh—no, I don't.[123] And don't

---

123 This time I knew where *my* phone was. It was on *my* bed. I think.

hit me." I thought I'd better say that, because she looked like she was thinking about it again.

Sara was wearing baggy jeans with about twenty-seven pockets.[124] She reached into one and pulled out a phone. "Allie's speed-dial four." Some people had been hanging around a few feet away, the way they do when they're waiting to talk to somebody. Sara turned to them. "Thanks, Max," she said over her shoulder.

I said, "No problem."

Then, to myself, I said, *Problem*.

---

124 Exaggeration reminder: "about twenty-seven pockets" is kind of funny—a little, anyway—but "about eight pockets" wouldn't be. You get it by now.

I have no idea how many pockets Sara's jeans actually had, but there were a lot. Maybe ninety.

chapter

PARKING TICKET; LITTLE BROTHER #1; LITTLE BROTHER #2

When Sara said that Allie wasn't coming, I'd been disappointed and relieved at the same time. I hadn't seen her in weeks, since school was out, and I wasn't sure if we were going to hang out together at the party, or what. One of the reasons I was relieved she wasn't coming was that we'd definitely have ended up slow dancing at least once, which I'd never done. I could just see myself stepping on her feet, and getting the beat all wrong and kind of staggering around with her.

That was also why I was disappointed she wasn't coming. I *wanted* us to end up slow dancing at least once, because, and I may as well tell you right here right now, I'd never put my arms around a girl and just held her,[125] like you get to do in a slow dance. I

---

125 Those stupid little hugs everybody gives each other don't count.

could imagine Allie pressed right up against me, her face so close, and her looking at me over those almost-invisible glasses.

So the way I was feeling was complicated.

But talking to her on the phone about how she wasn't at the party because of me turned out to be no problem after all, because she didn't answer.

"Did you leave a message?" Sara asked as I handed the phone back to her.

"Uhhhh . . . no."

"Max."

"I'll try later," I said. "I'm at a party, remember? Supposed to be having fun?"

She held out the phone to me again. "Don't forget." I took it back, put it in my pocket, and said I wouldn't.

"McNAUGHT'S HERE." That was Evan, a little while later. He had to shout because we were on the dance floor with a bunch of other people, going crazy. The music was fast and loud, and people were laughing and bumping into each other and laughing some more. The only daylight left was a smudge of light blue at the bottom of the sky. All the floodlights were off, and the yard was lit by tiny white bulbs on overhead wires I hadn't even noticed.

Evan and I were dancing with Gabrielle and Ava, the two softball girls, but Sara and a couple of other people were kind of dancing with us too. It was hard to tell, but it didn't matter. Maybe we were all so happy jumping around because each one of us had realized that it was going to be all right, that the party wouldn't be an embarrassing disaster after all.

Now all I had to do was avoid McNaught.

After a few songs there was a break. We were all half slumped over, breathing hard and still kind of laughing, when I saw a little kid weaving through the dance floor. His black hair was all spiky, and he was wearing a bright-red shirt that was so big on him that the shirttails went down almost to the bottom of his black shorts. Oh, and he had red socks. It was Sara's brother's friend—a ten-year-old goofball.

He walked right up to Gabrielle, pointed at her, and snapped his fingers. "Hey," he said, "are you a parking ticket?"

Gabrielle just stared at him. Stared *down* at him, I mean. She was a little taller than me, and this kid came up about to my shoulders. You could tell Gabrielle could hardly believe what she was seeing and hearing. "What?" she said. "What are you *talking* about?"

"You must be a parking ticket," he said, "because"—he pointed at her and snapped his fingers again—"you've got 'fine' written all over you."

No telling what Gabrielle was going to say to that, because Sara grabbed the kid by the elbow and spun him around, and was now hauling him toward the house.

"Alex is so dead," we heard her saying. "*So* dead."

"Alex is her little brother," I said to Gabrielle and Ava.

"What a shame," Evan said. "I always liked Alex."

"Yeah," I said. "I'll miss him."

A slow-dance song started up, and I sort of snuck off the dance floor. I even had an excuse—I was supposed to try to call Allie again.

I went into the house to get away from the music. Loud voices were coming from Alex's room: Sara yelling at Alex, Alex yelling at Sara that it wasn't his fault, and Mrs. Chen trying to get them to calm down. The only place I could think of that would be private enough and quiet enough for a phone call was the bathroom down the hall, but there was a strip of light coming from beneath the closed door. I leaned against the wall and waited.

"You guys were supposed to stay in here," I could hear Sara saying from Alex's room.

"What's the big deal?" That was the voice of the ten-year-old goofball. "Is there some law against dancing?"

"What do you want me to do, tie them both up?" Alex said.[126]

"All right," Mrs. Chen said. "You can fight about this tomorrow. Right now—"

Alex interrupted her. "And why did you have to invite *him*, anyway? He's such a loser. Just because you guys and his mother are—"

"Shhhhh!" Mrs. Chen said. "He'll hear you."

---

126 I'm not sure if this was eavesdropping or not. I mean, I wasn't there just so I could overhear what they were saying. But I guess I could have moved away, since it was a private conversation, or more like a private argument. This probably counts as half an eavesdrop.

"He's in the bathroom," said the goofball.

"What's the matter with you?" Mrs. Chen said. "He's your friend, and—"

"No, he's not. You're just always inviting him over here."

"Alex, you know that his father . . ."

Sara must have decided that her part of the argument was over, because she stomped out of the room and went back outside. She didn't even see me standing there down the hall. As she was walking away, the bathroom door opened. The boy came out and walked right by me on his way back to Alex's room, not looking at me. Just the way he'd walked to first base without looking at me after I hit him.

I was still leaning against the wall. "Whoa," I whispered.

Then I heard Mrs. Chen say, from Alex's room, "Hi, Lucas. Have you and Wiley been here for a while?"

Wiley? McNaught? *What?*

Then, all at once, it all made sense. This time I said it out loud.

"Whoa."

chapter

DARK SHADOWS; PASTA; MORE PASTA

What happened next didn't happen because Mad Max took over. There is no more Mad Max. I mean, there's no *separate* Mad Max. I realized why I'd been unable to find him: because I was looking around for him, when he'd already become a part of me. A new part of me, that is. I felt—no, I *knew* that I could do all kinds of things that I'd never been able to do before. But it would be *me* deciding what to do and what not to do, not this idea of a person called Mad Max.

My head was buzzing, and my arms and legs tingled as I walked down the hall to the party outside. McNaught was over by one of the long tables, talking to a couple of his buddies. He saw me come out of the house, stop, and motion with my head for him to meet me off in a far, dark part of the yard. I bet that of all the nine thousand things he could have imagined happening that night, this wasn't one of them.

I didn't even wait to see his reaction. I just went over and stood in the shadow of a big bush. He came walking up with his hands already in fists.

"Whadda you want?"

I was telling myself that as mean and messed up as McNaught was, he was still somebody who cared about stuff—like, his little brother.

"Am I a bad person?" I said.

He was surprised again. "What are you talking about, moron?" [27]

"Am I a bad person? Do I go around hurting people?" McNaught just stared at me. "The answer," I said, "is *no*. I do *not* go around hurting people. And I did *not* hit Lucas on purpose."

"Bull."

"It's the truth. Maybe some people pick on him, but not me. And I don't think *anybody* hit him on purpose. It was just this weird—"

"You're such a liar. Don't give me your crap. I was there. I saw you hit him. And now you don't like it 'cause I'm making you pay for it."

I said to myself, *This is hopeless.* I looked him dead in the eye. "It was an accident, *moron*." I turned around and walked back toward the party. "You can believe whatever," I called over my shoulder, "but leave me alone."

Everybody says that bullies are really cowards, and

---

27 Everybody keeps calling me that.
I hope it doesn't mean anything.

if you stand up to them, they back down. Everybody says that, but I think everybody's wrong. From what I've seen, bullies are mean jackasses who pick on people who are smaller than they are because they know that if those smaller people stand up to them, they can pound them into the ground in about four seconds. I just had to hope that I wouldn't find myself alone with McNaught for more than three seconds.[128]

And what had I thought was going to happen when I tried to talk to him? That he'd say he's sorry, and ask if I want to come over sometime to play Team Fortress 2? I don't want to be his friend anyway, because even though he may be more than just a mindless monster, even though he looks out for his little brother, I still really, really don't like him.

Now, as I reentered the party world, I saw McNaught's idiot friends messing around, trying to slap each other on the side of the head just like that idiot Connor used to do at camp. And it occurred to me that sometimes being a big, tough guy, not real smart, who people are kind of afraid of, and who hangs around with other big, tough guys who aren't real smart and who people are kind of afraid of, might not be all that much fun.

Sara's mom and dad and some other parents were bringing out food. There were gi-mongous pots of pasta and pasta sauce. They didn't go for our pizza idea, I guess. Right away there was a line almost all the way

---

128   And, as you know by now, I can tell <u>exactly</u> how long three seconds is.

around the yard. Evan was about in the middle, standing with Gabrielle and Ava. I moved toward the end, but Ava saw me and motioned for me to join them. I walked over, still in kind of a daze over what I'd said to McNaught. *Wow*, I was thinking. *I did it. I actually did it.*

"No cuts," said the guy in line behind them when I got there.

"Yes, cuts," Ava said. "Why not? Are you extra hungry? Are you afraid they're going to run out?" He looked away and didn't say anything else. Ava was like the exact opposite of Gabrielle—short, with short hair like Kim's, except Ava's is blond.

"Where'd you go, anyway?" she said. "I didn't have anybody to dance with."

It took about one-ninth of a second for the nervousness to kick in again. But it wasn't nearly as bad as I expected. After all, I had just dealt with McNaught. And I could feel that orange headband. It was part of me now.

"Can't tell you," I said, narrowing my eyes. "Secret mission."

"Max is a mysterious guy," Evan said. "He's always just disappearing."

Gabrielle laughed, but not in a mean way. "He doesn't look so mysterious to me."

"That's good," I said. "I try not to attract attention."[129]

---

129 I can't even remember most of the ridiculous stuff we said while we stood in line. It's the way you talk when you don't really know somebody, but you think you like them, and you hope they like you, and you're just sort of waiting until you've said enough words that you don't feel awkward anymore.

We got paper plates of pasta and heaped sauce on it, and dumped mountains of Parmesan cheese on top of that, and pretended we didn't see the salad, and grabbed cans of soda with bits of ice sliding down the sides, and looked around for a place to sit. There were still plenty of empty folding chairs, so we moved four of them over next to the dance floor. I was halfway concentrating on what people were saying and halfway concentrating on not splattering pasta sauce all over myself.

Sara carried a chair over and sat down. Gabrielle asked her if she'd killed Alex yet. "I'm going to wait a while," she said. "If I do it now, the police will come, and that'd be the end of the party."

"At least wait till after Extreme Musical Chairs," Evan said.

"After what?" Gabrielle and Ava said together.

It was going to work like this: Instead of having two lines of chairs back to back, like regular Musical Chairs, for Extreme Musical Chairs they'd be scattered all over the yard. Everybody would be dancing on the dance floor, and when the music stopped, we'd all have to make a mad dash for them.

"Fantastic," Ava said. "Chaos!"

"Maybe you should go ahead and kill Alex now," I said to Sara. "That way, when fights break out, the police will already be here."

"That's actually a pretty good idea," she said.

Extreme Musical Chairs started right after we were through eating. Most people were dancing, so the floor was incredibly crowded. Even McNaught was dancing, and even I could tell he had no idea what he was doing. He didn't seem to be hearing the music. I tried to feel sorry for him, but I didn't try very hard.

Anyway, the dance floor was jammed, but Ava and I weren't crowded at all. "Let's stay on the outside," she'd whispered to me before the first song. "That way we can get to the chairs faster." She'd gotten right up next to me as she whispered in my ear. It was so strange—she just *liked* me, right from the beginning. I wasn't thinking about Allie at all.

The music STOPPED! Ava and I jumped into two chairs that were a few feet away. Nobody had counted how many people were dancing, or how many chairs there were, and it turned out there were a lot fewer chairs than there were dancers. The very first song, a bunch of people got eliminated. By the third song only about ten people were still in, and the chairs that were left were all pretty far away and pretty far apart. I was hoping Ava would stay, so that the last song would be just the two of us dancing, with one chair left.

And it looked like that might happen. One song later only three people got chairs: Ava, me, and a guy named Christopher, one of Sara's zillion cousins.

The music came up again. Sara had moved the two remaining chairs to opposite ends of the yard. Christopher shouted to Ava, "You go for that chair over there, and—what's your name?"

"Max."

"Max and I will go for the other one."

"Got it," she said.

"Right," I said.

Ava was obviously dancing with me, which was very distracting and is why Christopher got a head start when the music STOPPED! again. Ava ran toward her chair. Christopher and I took off for the other one. I'm pretty fast, so I was thinking that once I got going, I'd fly right by him. And I did. Then I really started flying, because as I ran past a group of people, one of them, a guy named Wiley McNaught, stuck out his foot.

Everybody was yelling, and they yelled even louder when they saw me hit the ground and do about seventeen wild, flailing, half-sideways somersaults.[130] By the time I looked up, Christopher was almost to the chair. So no Extreme Musical Chairs last dance with Ava.

But not all the other chairs had been moved away, after all. I could just barely see the top of one, over on the other side of the food table. I scrambled to my feet and started running toward it as fast as I could.

"That chair counts!" I yelled, pointing to it as I ran. "It's in the yard! It counts!"

It took me just a few seconds to get to the table, wheel around the corner, and throw myself down on the chair. Remember how Sam sat down so fast on my sharpened pencil? Well, I sat down even faster than that. By the time I heard Evan yell "Max! No!," I'd figured out that somebody had left a plate of spaghetti on the chair because I could feel the thick sauce soaking through the back of my pants.[131]

---

130 Okay, more like two wild, flailing, half-sideways somersaults.

131 Finally. And it only took me 168 pages to get to it.

I jumped up. People standing around me screamed and hooted and pointed and yelled, "Omigod, omigod, you see that?" Other people ran over, shouting, "What? What happened?"

I didn't know where to go or what to do.

"This way, Max." Sara was pulling me by the arm toward a door in the side of the garage. "Secret passageway."

Plop! That was the paper plate falling off my butt and landing on the ground. People laughed even louder. Strands of spaghetti were falling from my butt and hitting the backs of my legs and ankles as Sara walked me toward the garage.

"I'm right behind you." That was Evan. I had the feeling we'd done this before.

Evan closed the door once we got into the garage, but I could still hear people laughing. Sara looked at me and sighed. "Max," she said, "are you all right?"

I didn't answer because I was in shock: I'd messed up the best night of my life. I wanted to shake my head really hard and wake myself up, but I knew it wouldn't work.[132]

The door opened and Ava peeked in. Oh, great. "What *happened*?" she said. She looked at me. "Did you really . . ." I turned a full circle, like I was a model. Ava clasped her hands over her mouth. Her eyes got *huge*. She started to laugh, and tried to smother it behind her hands.

"Thanks a lot," I said.

---

132 When you're dreaming, sometimes you don't know if it's a dream or if it's real. In real life, you <u>know</u> it's real.

"Hey," she said, "when somebody sits on a plate of spaghetti, it's funny."

It was quiet for a few seconds. Ava glanced over her shoulder, back toward the yard. "Uh, I have to do the last Extreme Musical Chairs thing. So . . ." She started backing out the door. "Maybe I'll see you later."

"Maybe," I said. The door closed. "Or maybe not." I tried to imagine what Allie would have done. She wouldn't have laughed at me, that's for sure. And she'd have been in here with Sara and Evan. It seemed strange that she wasn't.

Sara was walking around me, looking me up and down. "You know what, I've got a pair of sweatpants that might—"

Oh, yeah, like *that* was going to happen. "I think I'll just go," I said. I really wanted to be out of there.

"No, Max, don't," she said.

"Yeah," Evan said. "Come on. We'll think of something."

So we stood around and didn't think of anything at all.

"Party's going on without you," I finally said to Sara. Then, like I was a little boy with his mother standing over him, I said, "Thank you for inviting me."

"Well," she said, like she was a little girl, "thank you for coming." She looked at me and shook her head and smiled, and went back outside.

Evan followed her out. I waited till about the middle of the next song, then slipped out the door, went around to the back of the garage, climbed over a fence into a neighbor's yard, and headed for home.

chapter

THE MAN IN THE CAR;
MORE MISSING AIR;
LOOKING UP

After I made it down the neighbor's driveway and out to the sidewalk, I noticed that one of the cars parked on the street had its passenger-side window down. There was a man sitting behind the wheel, but not directly behind it—he was slumped over against the door. As I walked by, he mumbled, "Wiley." Then he half shouted, "Wiley!"

I bent down and looked in. He had his eyes mostly closed, but not quite—he was sort of squinting.

"Told you I'd be here. To pick you up. From your party." He was kind of mumbling, and slurring his words. "Can't blame a man for waiting for his boys . . ." He opened his eyes and looked right at me. "What?" he said. He started trying to sit up. "Who—" But I was already gone.

When I got to the corner, I turned to look back. McNaught was walking up to the car. It was under a streetlight and I wasn't, so he might not have seen me. I stood perfectly still, just like we'd all frozen in the moon shadows at camp. McNaught leaned in the car window.

Now was the time to move. I stepped behind another parked car and crouched down. What I needed to do was to keep low and slink away. What I did instead was peek around the side of the car.[133]

McNaught was leaning so far in that I couldn't even see his shoulders. Somebody was saying something, but I couldn't tell if it was him or his father—there were just little bursts of voice-sound.

They got louder. I couldn't understand anything, but there were two voices now, and both were shouting. McNaught pushed himself back from the car and stood up straight. Then he leaned back in and started screaming. I still couldn't make out the words, but there were some bad ones in there—you could tell. Then he stopped. He pushed himself back again, and turned and started walking down the sidewalk, fast. Straight toward me.

I looked around. No secret passageway. I thought about running down the driveway that was right there, then into the backyard, then into another backyard. I'd probably lose him. Or maybe I should just take off down the street and try to outrun him.

---

133 My dad says that if you want to spy on somebody, try to look around whatever you're hiding behind, because animals (that's us, too) notice things that pop up over the top of other things. I asked him where he learned that, and he said, "Spy school." But I think it's true anyway.

But then I pictured myself scampering away, a frightened little boy with a big bad bully after him. I could imagine hiding somewhere and trying not to breathe so loud. Or just running and running and running, constantly whipping my head around to see if he was gaining on me.

What I decided to do instead wasn't hard at all. Yesterday it might have been, but yesterday Mad Max was still a person outside of me, somebody I had to try to be. Not anymore. So what I did was, I stood up and stepped back onto the sidewalk.

McNaught came right up to me. I guess he'd known I was there all along.

"Having fun?" he said. "Gonna tell everybody about my drunk father passed out in his car?"

"No," I said, "I—"

Never saw it. The punch, I mean. I don't even know which fist he hit me with. I started talking, then something slammed into my mouth, just *POW!*—like that. My head snapped back. He hadn't hit me that hard, but it was right in the mouth, and I could feel blood dripping down my chin, and I could taste it on my teeth. When I put both hands up to my mouth, he hit me in the stomach.[134] It totally knocked the breath out of me. If that's ever happened to you, you know it means that you really can't breathe at all. I twisted away as I was falling down to my knees, gasping, but it was more like gulping because no air was coming in.

---

134 This is taking twenty times longer to tell than it did to happen.

I think that's when he hit me on the side of the head, just in front of my left ear, but I'm not sure. All I know is that next I was on the ground, curled up, covering my head, still not able to breathe, and McNaught was hitting me in the side, in the ribs, in the back. He was yelling at me, but I don't know what he was saying—I could just tell that it was like he was so mad, he couldn't stand it. A light went on, a door opened, a man's voice yelled, "Hey!" and McNaught was gone.

"Are you all right? Son? Are you all right?"

The same voice. Then somebody else, a woman, was saying, "I think we should call the police."

I was lying on my right side in their front yard, still curled up, trying to get back some of the air I'd been missing.

"Son?"

"I think we should call the police," the woman said again. The man helped me get up. The light was behind them, so I couldn't see their faces very well, but I could tell they were old, and that they were upset and scared.

"No, I'm okay," I said, and I was. It didn't feel like I was bleeding anymore, or at least not as much, and I could breathe again. I felt sore in a bunch of places, but not really injured or anything.

"Are you sure?" the man said.

I nodded, and noticed some drops of blood on my shirt. Funny how that kept happening.

"That's good," he said. "But we really should call—"

"No, don't, please," I said. "It's just . . . I mean, I

know him, and we sort of have a . . . Anyway, I can handle it. Really."

"Well," the woman said, "we can at least call your parents. Why don't you come inside and—"

"Oh, no thanks, no." I wasn't going to be the poor little boy with an OW-ie, waiting for his mommy and daddy to come pick him up and wipe his nose and tell him everything was going to be all right. "I was on my way home anyway. And I'm okay now."

They really wanted to do something for me, but I couldn't wait to start walking—to just be by myself. I backed away.

"Bye," I said. "Thanks for coming out." I gave them a sort of half wave, and they both gave me one back.

It took me about half an hour to get home. A few people were out walking their dogs, but it was so dark—no moon—that I didn't worry about anybody seeing the back of my spaghetti pants, except right under a street-light and every now and then when a car came up from behind. Just before the headlights would catch up to me, I'd turn halfway around and wait until the car went by. But most of the time it was just me, walking block after block.

The left side of my head was throbbing, and I had the start of a headache, because McNaught had hit me there pretty hard. I tried to remember the last time I was in a fight, if just getting beaten up even counts as a fight. When I was little, neighborhood fights meant you'd wrestle around with some guy until one of you was on top and could pin the other guy's wrists to the ground, and he'd struggle and struggle until he started crying and somebody's mother or father came out. Maybe you'd slug each other in the arms or in the stomach, but hardly ever did anybody get hit in the face. Now I was in the big time, I guess.

Anyway, I was sore but not hurt bad or anything, and after a few minutes I realized that I was having an amazing time. These were streets I'd walked along and ridden my bike on and seen through the window of a car my whole life, but everything seemed way different. Well, not different, really. It's that I was noticing so many things. I could see every leaf on every tree that was lit by a streetlight. There was hardly any wind, and when a car would whoosh by me, I'd really *feel* the breeze.

Even walking was like it never had been before. When my feet hit the ground, left, right, left, right, I pushed off with every step and drove myself forward. I was moving myself through the world, instead of being this boy who's dragged around and carried from place to place. I looked down and saw the sidewalk racing under my footsteps. I was *going* somewhere.

Then our house was up ahead, on the right. I saw it coming nearer, like I was a movie camera zooming in. Sidewalk, right turn just past the mailbox, up the concrete path, stop, key, open the door, in.

The TV was on in the den, so I was able to make it through the house and into the bathroom without anybody seeing me. I could have changed my clothes and asked my mom or dad or Ben, if he was home, to drive me back, but by then there probably wasn't much party left. Not that I felt like going back anyway.

My lip wasn't nearly as big or cut as badly as it felt like it was, but the left side of my face, up near my eye, was already a little purple. My head was really starting to hurt, so I took a couple of ibuprofen. Then I washed the blood off my chin, opened the door and looked up and down the hall to make sure nobody was around, and made it safely to my room. My mom must have heard me, though.

"Party over already?" she said through the door.

"Yup." I was pulling off my bloody shirt.

"Who gave you a ride home?"

"Walked." I tossed the shirt into the dirty clothes corner.

Pause.

"Are you all right?"

"Yup."

Long pause.

"Max?"

"What?"

"I'm coming in." She opened the door. "I want to know what—"

I turned around to show her my spaghetti-butt pants. "Go ahead and laugh," I said. "Everybody thinks it's hilarious."

I looked over my shoulder to see if she really was going to laugh, but she saw my face, and gave a little jump and gasped. "Oh, Max," she said, or more like, breathed out. "What—" She started to come in, but I held up a STOP! sign with my hands, both palms out. She stopped.

"Is it okay if we don't talk about it now?" I said.

"Did you get into a fight? Who hit you? Max, I want you to tell me who—I'm going to get your father."

"Mom, no! Please!" She turned back. "Really, I'm fine. We can all talk about it tomorrow, and I'll tell you about how I sat on the plate of spaghetti—"

"So that's what that stuff is."

"—and about how the stupid fight was no big deal. Then you and Dad can tell me that someday I'll look back and laugh about the whole thing. Please?"

We stared at each other for four or five seconds. I don't think you need a footnote here to tell you that's a long time.

"Okay. I guess . . . well . . . okay." She backed out of the room. "Sure. We can talk about it tomorrow. And I'll try to remember to say that someday you'll laugh about the whole thing. You can remind me if I forget." She closed the door.

I kicked off my sneakers and stepped out of my pants slowly, so as not to get pasta sauce on anything. When I balled up the pants to throw them in the corner, I felt something in one of the pockets.

Sara's phone.

I put on some jeans and a clean shirt, then took a big book from the shelf, pulled back the curtain in front of my bed,[135] climbed in, closed the curtain, and

---

135 Another advantage to having a curtain there is that I never have to make the bed.

snapped on the reading light. I sat there for a while, cross-legged, with the book on my lap, flipping though pictures and descriptions of scientific equipment.

Something moved. Alice's feet were hitting the bottom of the curtain—she was asleep and dreaming. I put the book aside and climbed out. "C'mon, girl," I said.

We walked out into the backyard. I sat in a lawn chair.[136] Alice turned a couple of circles and flopped down to go back to whatever doggie dream I'd interrupted. Ever since I'd hit her and thought she was dead, she'd made me happier than she ever had before. I'd look at her, and she'd remind me of all the bad things that could happen but don't. Now I was sitting outside in the dark with her, after this great party turned out to be a disaster that I'll remember till I'm 103, and after Wiley McNaught beat the crap out of me.

I was feeling pretty bad, but in an incredibly good way. I know that sounds strange. What I mean is, I liked it that real stuff was happening in my life.

I liked it *a lot.*

For a while I went back and forth between watching the sky and watching Alice sleep. Then I took out the phone and punched speed-dial 4.

"Hi, Sara," Allie said. "Don't worry, I'm all right."

"Hey, Allie. It's me."

She didn't say anything at first. Then she sighed. "Hi, Max."

"Wait till you hear this."

---

136 Yes.

And I told her all about the Extreme Musical Chairs Disaster, and how Sara and Evan had come to the rescue just like we'd rescued her at the mall. I knew that I'd better not say much about Ava. That made me kind of stumble around a couple of times. But I must have told the story pretty well,[137] because pretty soon she was laughing, and I was laughing too. The "someday" that I'd think it was funny—the spaghetti-butt part, not the McNaught-beating-me-up part; I didn't tell her about that—had come a lot sooner than I expected.

Except that when I finished, I realized that what I was hearing now was Allie crying. I felt a stabbing ache deep in the middle of my chest, right about where they say your heart is.

"Allie?" I said. "What's the matter?"

She wouldn't answer. I waited, trying again, for what seemed like the twentieth time tonight, to think of the right thing to say. But it was strange—Allie's crying was also making me feel warm and good, because even though we were having a really bad night, and we both felt humiliated, it didn't seem all that awful because we were having a bad night and feeling humiliated together.

So that's what I said to her.

"I can't even describe exactly how I feel," I said. "But I know you kind of know what I mean."

She'd stopped crying by then. She just sounded sad.

---

137 All right, I exaggerated a little as I was telling it. So what? It's a story, right?

"I *do* know what you mean," she said. "But I'm just so confused and miserable. I wanted to come to the party, I really did, but I *couldn't*, and—"

"Shooting star," I said.

She sniffled. "What?"

"I'm sitting in the backyard, and I saw a shooting star."

"Oh."

"Where are you right now?"

"In my room."

"Go to the window and look up. There are a lot of shooting stars this time of year."

"Okay." There were sounds of her moving around. "It's really dark tonight," she said.

"Yeah. No moon."

"Max, I *wanted* to come—"

"It's okay."

"Really, I—"

"It's *okay*," I said. "Well, I guess I could have used your help covering up my butt . . ."

Soft laughter. It sounded *so* good.

". . . but aside from that, it's okay. These days I don't know who I am or what I'm doing half the time either."

We stopped talking, but we stayed on the phone for a while anyway. It was nice just to sit out there with the phone to my ear, looking at the night sky. Every now and then I could hear Allie breathing.

"Shooting star," I said.

"Shooting star," she said.

chapter

22.5

ANYWAY,

Anyway, that's how I ended up sitting on a plate of spaghetti.

But now that I've gone to all this trouble to tell you the story, I get the feeling that it isn't even *about* sitting on a plate of spaghetti. And it's not about secret passageways, or baseball, or lawn chairs, or being nice to waitresses, or what it's like to get beaten up. Or even about how important it is to tread softly in this place.

No, if you get only one thing out of reading my book, this should be it. Are you ready? Are you paying attention? Good. Here it is:

Never, ever, *ever* put a sharpened pencil under somebody's butt.[138]

---

138 The end.